The little photo the murderer held against the glass window of Cell Number 17 was of Jay's daughter. Jenny's first-grade school picture. The one that only looked decent because Sandra had worked half an hour combing their daughter's hair so that unsightly gap in her bangs wouldn't show. The photo Jenny had brought home in the picture package, in her backpack, yesterday afternoon.

"Where the hell did you get that?" Jay pulled his wallet frantically from his back pocket and unfolded it. The plastic window that had held his daughter's photo a few hours before was empty.

"Such a pretty little girl. Too bad about that stutter. I hear Danny Torello has been giving her a hard time about it. 'J-J-J-Jennifer!' he calls her. Bullying is such an ugly thing, don't you think?"

Suddenly, the key was in the lock and Jay was wrenching the metal door open. All precaution and common sense had flown completely out the window. He had to have that photo and he sure as hell was going to find out how the bastard got it out of his wallet.

Jay slipped the nightstick from his belt and took a firm grip on it. Hacker was no longer standing where he had been before. He was in the dark cell somewhere. Jay reached over with his free hand and found the light switch. He turned it on. Nothing happened. The cell remained as black as pitch.

"Hacker," he said, trying to keep his voice calm and even. "Where are you, Hacker?"

Step out and shut the door... now! he told himself. But the photograph. He had to have...

There was a tug and his belt grew eight ounces lighter.

First Edition

VAULT

OF

SOUTHERN-FRIED

HORROR

RONALD KELLY

CONTENTS

BREAKFAST SERIAL

Chester Freely had been kicking around the dusty rural backroads of northern Alabama for many days, and early that Saturday morning he sat down to breakfast with a charming farm family by the name of Johnson.

"Danged fine cook, my Emma... don't you think so, boy?" beamed Fred Johnson contentedly. He pushed away from the table and patted his swollen belly.

"Oh, yes, sir," Chester agreed. He gave Mrs. Johnson an appreciative smile. "Best home-cooked meal I've had in quite a while, ma'am."

"Glad you enjoyed it, young man. More biscuits and molasses with your coffee?"

"No, thanks. I'm stuffed."

The twins, Randy and Rita, waved empty jelly-jar glasses at their mother. "Can we have some more chocolate milk, Mama? Please?"

Emma Johnson eyed them in a moment of indecision, then broke into a smile. "Well, maybe just one more glass won't hurt none." She walked toward the refrigerator at the other side of the kitchen.

"I sure appreciate you helping me mend that fence along the south pasture this morning," said Fred. He had already milked the cows and slopped the hogs, when Chester had wandered up the road and offered to lend a hand.

"My pleasure," nodded the lanky drifter. "Kinda hard to find good honest work when you're on the road as much as I am. Sure glad to help out folks whenever I can."

The Johnsons smiled at their guest, unaware of the secret he held. A secret that he concealed well behind a handsome, good-natured smile of his own.

Chester Freely was a serial killer.

He had been at it nearly three years now and, by his count, had murdered nearly twenty-two families—families very much like the Johnsons. He committed one every couple of months, sometimes two if he found the opportunity. And he never murdered in the same state twice in a row. He would do one in Minnesota, then one in California, another in Texas, still another in Maine. He staggered them out across the country, never leaving a definite pattern, never performing his atrocities in exactly the same manner. Perhaps that was why the authorities hadn't wised up to him yet. Either that or pure dumb luck.

Now he was sitting in a cheerful kitchen in a lonely farmhouse twenty miles north of Birmingham. He liked the South almost as much as he liked the Midwest, for it was there where his victims lived in great abundance. The requirements were always the same—a hard-working, God-fearing farmer and his modest family who lived on acreage so vast that his closest neighbor lived quite a ways down the road. In other words, a small group of people who were totally isolated in their everyday routine. Sometimes his victims were so far out in the sticks that they weren't discovered for several days. By then he was three or four states way, satisfied for the moment, but secretly contemplating his next massacre.

Chester was rarely treated to such a fine meal as the one Emma Johnson had prepared that morning. After saying grace, they dug in. Scrambled eggs, country-cured ham, big cathead biscuits, and all the black coffee he could drink. At first, he had nearly considered letting this one pass, but decided otherwise. It was nearing the end of the month and he was desperately in need of the physical and emotional rush that wholesale murder gave him. The gruesome sight of blood and mutilation intoxicated him much like some potent drug, placing him in the same category as a junkie in constant search of a fix.

A faint whimper and a scratching at the back door drew their attention. Chester grinned. He had been mulling over his execution of today's bloodletting all during breakfast and now it came to him, suddenly and without warning, almost causing him to laugh out loud.

"Mrs. Johnson, do you mind if I carve off a slab of this ham for my dog?" Chester asked politely. "He hasn't had a bite since yesterday." He had started traveling with a dog during his second year. Mostly he would befriend some stray he came across while he was on the road. People seemed to trust strangers more easily when they traveled with a dog. Besides, whenever he got tired of them and needed a cheap thrill, Chester just slaughtered the poor mutts, then tossed them in a ditch or stuffed them in a drainage pipe. But it was never the same as doing it to a human being.

Emma smiled at her guest warmly. "Why, certainly you can! But let me get you a sharper knife. That one there is kind of dull." She began to rummage through a counter drawer.

"I'd sure appreciate it," said Chester calmly. He was so wired now that he could barely sit still. He glanced around the table. Fred Johnson sat back, his belt loosened a few notches, thumbing through a copy of the local, small-town paper. The Johnson children giggled at the sad-eyed dog that peered through the screen door, chocolate milk mustaches splashed broadly beneath their pert, little noses.

Emma Johnson started across the spotless linoleum floor, holding the large butcher knife by its wooden handle. "Here you go, young man. Be careful. It's sharp."

He had it all worked out now. As soon as he had his fingers wrapped around the haft of the knife, he would turn and sink it deep into Fred's solar plexus, killing him instantly. Emma would stand there stunned for a second, long enough for him to grab that antique iron skillet that hung beside the nick-nack shelf and brain her enough to knock her flat. He didn't want her dead just yet. Emma was a drab, homely woman, but she had a nice body. She would be repeatedly tortured and humiliated before he allowed her to join her husband in death.

By the time their mother hit the floor, Randy and Rita would react in one of two ways. They would either sit there in shock or they would run screaming for their lives. He hoped for the latter. It was always so much fun hunting children, like a hound running a coon. They all had the mistaken notion that they could hide from him. Sometimes it was under a bed, sometimes behind a tree outside or in the hayloft of the barn. The Johnson twins had been so polite and loveable throughout his stay, that he figured they were deserving of something special. A beheading perhaps. Yes, either that or dismemberment.

This is going to be easy, Chester thought. *So damned easy.*

As his perfect hostess approached the table, he reached out, the hairs on the nape of his neck tingling with anticipation. "Thank you very much, Mrs.—"

He didn't get a chance to finish his statement. With an upward swipe, sweet Emma Johnson slit his throat from ear to ear.

Chester Freely fell backward out of his chair, an expression of utter surprise dawning on his pale face. He hit hard, splattering blood across the linoleum tiles. His *own* blood!

He wanted to say, *"What the hell is going on?"* but that was quite impossible. The blade had sliced clean through his larynx, as well as the major arteries. The only sound that he could make was a wet gurgling as blood engorged his severed windpipe.

Then the children were upon him. Little Randy and Rita laughed playfully, running around the leg of the oaken table with sharp implements. They attacked his abdomen with a bloodlust he himself had rarely possessed. Randy jabbed at him with a butter knife, while pig-tailed Rita impaled him viciously again and again with a fork from Emma's best silverware.

"That's enough, kids," laughed Emma, crouching down to hug her bloodstained babies. "He's dead now."

"Look, Papa!" the twins squealed as one. "Look, Papa, look!"

Fred Johnson arched his eyebrows and puffed on his pipe. "My, my, now ain't that a fine piece of work," he said proudly. "Couldn't have done it better myself."

Emma stared down at the butchered body lying across her kitchen floor. "Such a nice young man. Sure wish we could've let him go this time."

"Now, Emma," said Fred, stretching lazily. "You know very well if we let one go, it'd have to go for 'em all."

The woman sighed. "I suppose so. Where are we gonna put this one? The root cellar?"

"Nah, we've got them stacked like cord wood down there already. I reckon we oughta start stashing them in the smokehouse now." Fred winked at his young'uns. "I'll tell you kids what. You two help me carry this fellow outside and we'll clean up and drive into town for ice cream afterwards. How does that sound?"

"Oh boy!"

"Yippee!"

The children's blood-speckled faces broke into broad grins as they each grabbed ahold of one of Chester's trouser legs and began to pull him toward the back door.

END OF SHIFT

Jay Wilmore stood at the guard's station on the east wing of Floor Three—the most dangerous ward in the building, or so he had been told—as the veteran guard on duty checked him in. It was his first night on the job and, Jay had to admit, his nerves were wired to the max.

"I would be neighborly and say something like 'welcome'," Sam Prater offered, "but everyone we welcome here are the sort of guests who never end up leaving." He nodded toward the long corridor that stretched beyond the safety barrier. Jay stared through the sturdy, iron bars at the brightly-lit hallway. The walls were painted a sickly sea-foam green and along the walls on either side were heavy, steel doors with a single window set at face level. From right to left, there were sixteen in all. And, at the very end of the dead-end corridor, was Number 17.

That was the one that bothered Jay Wilmore the most.

Sam sensed the young man's unease. "Don't sweat it. You'll do just fine. Just keep on your toes and try not to fraternize with the inmates, and this job will be a piece of cake. Oh, you'll see and hear a lot of crazy shit…" Officer Prater caught himself. "Sorry… we're not supposed to use that word. You'll hear a lot of *mentally unbalanced* shit… but don't pay it any attention. Leave it here on Floor Three when you clock out and go home to your family with a clear mind." He regarded Jay—tall and lean, scarcely twenty-five years old—and was curious. "You are married, aren't you?"

The new guard smiled. "Yep. For six years now. Got a beautiful wife and a little girl, four years old. All blue eyes and curly, blonde hair. Whatever she wants, she gets from dear old Dad."

Sam chuckled. "I got a couple like that myself, but they're halfway through college now. I'm not going to lie, though. They still have me twisted around their little fingers the same as they did the day they were born."

Laughter echoed from down the green corridor. From the door at the very end.

"You keep looking at Number 17."

"Well, it's kind of hard not to," admitted Jay. "That's the one, isn't it? The one *he's* in?"

Sam took the new man by the elbow and turned him away from the steel-barred gate and the ward that lay just beyond. "Listen to me, son. It kinda bothers me...you starting your first day acting like some kind of true crime fanboy." The elder guard glanced over Jay's shoulder. In the little window of Door Number 17, a face grinned through the reinforced glass. It looked like a framed portrait of pure, unbridled lunacy. "None of these guys here deserve special attention... not for what they've done... especially not *that* one."

Jay's ears reddened in embarrassment. "I'm just curious, that's all."

The middle-aged man nodded, not looking at all convinced. "So, you haven't read the three books written about him... or seen the Netflix special?"

"Well, yeah... all of that."

Sam looked him square in the eyes. The stare was so intense, he had the young guard's undivided attention. "Take my advice, kid. Don't go down there if you don't have to. Don't look at him... and sure as hell don't *talk* to him. It's better for you and all of us if you just keep your distance and treat him like any other nutcase in the ward. Don't give him what he wants. Don't treat him like a celebrity."

Jay knew he should just keep his mouth shut, but his wife always told him that he had about as much tact as a skeleton has spit. "Well, in a way, he *is*, isn't he?"

Sam shook his head in wonder. "You're not earning any brownie points this morning, you know that? Now, I hate to pull rank on you—I'm really not that kind of guy—but I *am* your superior. And I'm telling you to keep your ass away from him. You don't want him in your head, or everything he can weasel out of you inside his. He's insane, but he isn't dumb. In fact, he's probably smarter than me and you put together."

Jay sensed that he had been walking on thin ice. "I'm sorry, sir. I didn't mean to start out on the wrong foot."

The elder guard smiled and clapped Jay on the shoulder. "Let's just forget it and start fresh. I'll show you the ropes this week and then you go on nights the next. Most of the inmates will sleep through your eight-hour shift and you won't even know they're there." Again, he looked down the corridor to the end. "Except him. It's like he's up twenty-four/seven. He never sleeps."

Jay Wilmore wanted to turn around and see if that grinning face was still in the window of Door Number 17. Wanted to know if he was watching and listening. But he didn't. He knew he had pushed his luck too far already.

A couple of days later, Jay was sitting at a table in the cafeteria downstairs when someone slid into a chair opposite him. It was a fellow guard, more heavy in gut than muscle, and sporting a thick brown beard. Jay had seen him around the facility for the criminally insane, but didn't know his name.

"You don't mind if I sit here, do you?" he asked, unwrapping a tuna salad sandwich he had bought from a vending machine.

"No, go ahead." He took a bite of his own ham and cheese.

"Jay Wilmore."

"Ted McNair," answered the other. "So, how do you like it here?"

Jay shrugged. "It's a job."

Ted nodded. "Same here. I guess there's worse ways to draw a paycheck, huh?" He opened a bag of chips and ate a couple. "You're on Floor Three, aren't you?"

"Yeah."

"Where all the high-octane squirrels are. So, have you seen *him* yet?"

Jay tried to act like he didn't know what he was talking about. "Seen *who?*"

Ted rolled his eyes. "You know who! Big daddy of the block. Hoyt Hacker."

Jay's heart felt like it skipped a beat. He believed that was the first time he had actually heard the man's name spoken out loud since he got there.

The other guard snickered. "Hacker! The name fits, don't you think?"

Jay looked at the big man across from him, sensing that he was someone he could talk to without it getting back to Sam Prater. "I know. You don't think his name being that, you know, triggered something?"

Ted smiled. "You never know with guys like that. One moment they're as sane as you or me. The next, they're hacking away at their family with a freaking axe."

Jay suddenly didn't feel as hungry as he had a moment before. "Yeah… them and everyone else in the neighborhood."

"Seventeen in all, wasn't it? Jesus, even kids. And one a baby just home from the hospital."

Now Jay definitely didn't have an appetite. "Did they ever figure out why he did it?"

"No," said Ted, "and he's never said either. He's a damn enigma. I guess most looney tunes like that are. Only, he's got a Wikipedia page and fifty pages of links on Google."

Jay stood up and gathered his trash from the tabletop. "Well, I guess I'd better get back to my station. It was nice talking to you, Ted."

"Yeah, bro. Same here." Before Jay could step away, Ted reached out and grabbed his arm. "Uh, hey, be careful, okay? Three other guys have had your job and they didn't last a week. And it all had to do with *him*."

"I'll be alright," Jay assured him. "I know how to handle myself."

Ted's smile told him that he wasn't a hundred percent convinced. "Yeah, right. Well… see you around."

Jay nodded and, dumping his garbage in a trash can, headed upstairs to continue his shift.

Everything was fine for his first three nights on third shift. Until Thursday.

Then it happened.

He was walking down the long hallway beyond the barred security area, checking doors, making sure they were secure. When he reached Door 17, the window was dark. No light inside.

Jay felt relieved. Maybe he did sleep after all. He checked the door and, satisfied that it was locked, turned to go.

"Hey, new guy. Let's talk."

The guard stopped in his tracks. It was the voice. The one on the interviews, the interrogation videos, the loop track in the middle of that song by that death metal band. What was the name of it? "Hacker Hoyt on Bloodstained Avenue" … a play on Bloomstead Avenue, the street where all those friends and neighbors had innocently opened their doors and received an axe blade through the forehead or across their throat.

He took a couple steps, trying to ignore him.

"Come on… you've been wanting to talk to me. It's been eating at you since you received the call that you got the job."

Jay stopped and sighed. *Don't do this. Just leave well enough alone.* But he couldn't.

He turned and looked at the little window. Hoyt Hacker had his face pressed all the way up to the glass, so much so that the flesh of his forehead, nose, and cheeks were flattened and distorted. Along with that wicked, mile-wide grin of his, Hacker looked more like some obscene cartoon character than an actual human being.

"Yeah, Hacker? What do you want?" He tried to sound unconcerned, nonchalant. But under his uniform shirt his heart was beating like a jackhammer.

The inmate laughed. "Whoa, buddy. Slow that ticker down. I ain't gonna hurt you. I'm in here and you're out there. No need to piss your pants."

"Don't flatter yourself," Jay said, attempting to keep his voice steady and authoritative. "Now just shut up and get back to… well, whatever you were doing."

"What I was doing was waiting for you, Jay," said Hacker. "I just wanted to talk. Don't you want to talk? Maybe ask me some questions? You do have them, don't you? Questions?"

Something bothered the young guard. How had he known his first name? His name tag only said Wilmore. "No, I don't have any questions. I really don't give a shit about you or why you're in here."

Hacker laughed. It sent a shiver down Jay's spine. He sort of felt like Batman with the Joker standing a few feet away.

"Liar, liar, pants on fire!" taunted the mass murderer. "Come on. I'm bored. I'll tell you anything you want to know. You tell me something, I tell you something in return. Sound like a fair deal?"

He heard Sam Prater's words in his mind. *You don't want him in your head, or everything he can weasel out of you inside his.*

"Sorry. No time for talking. I've got to get back to my desk. Got things to take care of." He turned and started back down the hall.

"Like playing Wordle on your phone? Or is it Candy Crush?" Hacker giggled. "Sandra would kid the living shit out of you if she knew you played that, wouldn't she?"

Sandra? How did he know about Sandra?

"There goes your heart again. Boom-ba-boom-ba-boom. You're gonna have a coronary before you reach your twenty-sixth birthday, buddy. It's on the twenty-ninth, isn't it?"

Against his better judgment, Jay whirled on his heels and glared at the face in the window. "How the hell do you know...?"

Hacker displayed that stupid grin of his, but didn't laugh. This time, his eyes didn't match the smile below it. They were bright and shiny, almost feverish. Like a Peeping Tom. Except he was spying on the guard's thoughts and not some naked woman through a bathroom window.

"I don't know nothing, fella. You're a big mystery to me. But not for long. You'll talk to me... and it won't be long, either."

Get the hell out of here, Jay told himself. He turned back around, walked to the end of the corridor, unlocked the barred gate, and then closed it behind him.

"Go on!" yelled Hacker behind him. "It's almost lunch time. Eat that chicken salad sandwich on honey wheat bread with the sour cream and onion chips. And the Little Debbie oatmeal pie for dessert."

Jay walked to his desk a couple of yards from the gate. On his desk was his Igloo cooler. Inside was chicken salad on honey wheat, a bag of sour cream and onion chips, and an oatmeal pie. He hadn't seen what Sandra had packed him for lunch... she had told him it was a surprise.

But it wasn't. He knew they were there.

Just as Hoyt Hacker had told him.

The following Monday night, Jay was sitting at his desk, filling out inmate evaluations, when Hacker's voice drifted down the hallway. He was singing that song... the one about Bloodshed Avenue.

"Shut up down there, Number 17!" Jay told him, loud enough for the inmate to hear.

The singing stopped. "Oh, we're going by numbers now, are we? So I can call you 8043, then? Or 1277? Which one do you prefer?"

Jay felt sick to his stomach. The first one was the last four digits of his Social Security number... the second the last four of his cell phone number.

I've had enough of this shit, he thought to himself. *I've got to know how he's finding these things out.*

He stood up and, before approaching the gate, checked his belt. Everything was in place. The pepper spray, nightstick, and taser. He wasn't intending on opening the door of Number 17, but he wanted to know they were there, in case... *what?* What was he afraid of? Hacker was just a man behind six inches of steel security door. There was no threat to him at all.

A minute later, Jay was standing at the end of the hall, facing Hoyt Hacker's cell. "I want to know how you...?"

"What? Know that your mom's favorite flowers are purple iris? Sandra's dream vacation is Venice, Italy?" Hacker grinned broadly and held something up to the little window. He held it against the glass, so Jay had no trouble seeing it. "Or that Jennifer almost screwed up this picture because she got ahold of the scissors in the kitchen drawer by the refrigerator and decided to cut her own hair?"

The little photo the murderer held against the glass was of Jay's daughter. Jenny's first-grade school picture. The one that only looked decent because Sandra had worked half an hour combing their daughter's hair so that unsightly gap in her bangs wouldn't show. The photo Jenny had brought home in the picture package, in her backpack, yesterday afternoon.

"Where the hell did you get that?" Jay pulled his wallet frantically from his back pocket and unfolded it. The plastic window that had held his daughter's photo a few hours before was empty.

"Such a pretty little girl. Too bad about that stutter. I hear Danny Torello has been giving her a hard time about it. 'J-J-J-Jennifer!' he calls her. Bullying is such an ugly thing, don't you think?"

Suddenly, the key was in the lock and Jay was wrenching the metal door open. All precaution and common sense had flown completely out the window. He had to have that photo and he sure as hell was going to find out how the bastard got it out of his wallet.

Jay slipped the nightstick from his belt and took a firm grip on it. Hacker was no longer standing where he had been before. He was in the dark cell somewhere. Jay reached over with his free hand and found the light switch. He turned it on. Nothing happened. The cell remained as black as pitch.

"Hacker," he said, trying to keep his voice calm and even. "Where are you, Hacker?"

Nothing. Complete silence. Not even the sound of breathing.

Step out and shut the door... now! he told himself. But the photograph. He had to have...

There was a tug and his belt grew eight ounces lighter.

"Dance for me, new guy."

Then a *pop* and the jab of barbs in his chest. And the sizzle of voltage traveling through the lead wires from taser to flesh.

A moment later, Jay was on the floor, jerking and bucking, and pissing his pants.

And the occupant of Number 17 was at the opposite end of the hall, slamming the security gate behind him, laughing all the way.

"Let's go over this again, Officer Wilmore."

"But I told you..."

"Again, Wilmore. Give us the reason. Why the hell did you open that door?"

He was in the warden's office, sitting in a chair in the center of the room. Still jittery from the tasing, sweating profusely, nervous as hell. There were nine other people in the room with him—Warden Thompson, Sam Prater, two guards (Ted, that he had met in the cafeteria and another named Henry), the chief of police and a patrol officer, a legal assistant from the district attorney's office, and two FBI agents. None of them were happy. They had a lot on their plate early that morning.

After all, their most infamous inmate had flown the coop and had been on the loose for the past four hours.

"He… he had my daughter's photograph. I told you that already."

"And how did he gain possession of it, Officer Wilmore?" asked one of the FBI agents. A thin woman with her dark hair pinned back and a severe look on her narrow face. "Are you sure it's not still in your wallet?"

"Hell, no, it's not in my wallet!"

"Could you check for us?"

"Okay!" Angrily, he took the wallet from his hip pocket. "But it's not…"

"Just humor us. Please."

Jay opened the wallet. Daddy's little girl smiled at him from behind the plastic window.

"How the hell did this get—"

Now it was the warden's turn. "Officer Wilmore, you are hereby suspended from duty until an inquiry takes place concerning this grave breech of security." He shook his balding head angrily. "Dammit, man… how could you let this happen?"

"I… I'm sorry."

"Prater, take his belt and equipment, and then escort him from the building. We will be in touch with you, Officer Wilmore." There was no leniency in the warden's voice. Just stern coldness lacking any degree of mercy whatsoever.

Ten minutes later, he was at the time clock. His superior watched in sullen silence as he clocked out and returned his card to its place in the slot rack on the wall.

"This isn't looking good for you, Wilmore," Prater finally said with a sigh. "I warned you, didn't I?"

Jay said nothing, just left the building and walked across the parking lot to his car. Feeling stunned and confused, wondering exactly how—and why—he had let his guard down and allowed one of the country's most notorious mass murderers walk away from a maximum-security facility, scot-free.

Jay pulled his car into the driveway and sat there for a long moment, still trying to digest what had taken place. He was afraid to go in the house. What would Sandra say about all this? He could already see the worry and disappointment in her pretty face.

Finally, he sighed, climbed out, and walked up the sidewalk to the front door. It was a little after eight-thirty. He usually got home from his shift a quarter after six. Jenny would already be at school and his wife would be in her office, working from home.

He reached for the doorknob.

The door swung slowly open.

Somewhere inside, someone laughed. *He* laughed.

Oh no... oh God.

Jay reached to his belt and found... nothing. No nightstick, no pepper spray, no taser. They were on Sam Prater's desk back at the facility.

Scarcely able to breathe, he pushed the door all the way open. Stepped in. Felt the carpet go squishy under the soles of his shoes. Soaked full of...

"Come in and join the party, Jay."

The first thing he saw was Sandra. She was over there... and here... and *everywhere.*

Hoyt Hacker stood in the center of the living room. His orange coveralls were dark red now. Glistening. His face happy. His hair full of blood and gore and tiny bits of Sandra.

"Daddy's home," the man said softly. "Run and give him a big kiss." And, with that, he slung something in Jay's direction. Something he had been holding in his bloody hand. Something pale and round, with long honey-blonde hair.

As it rolled toward him, Jay saw everything. The freckles. The hole in her smile where she had lost a baby tooth a week ago. The glassy blue eyes. The gap in her bangs caused by the scissors.

Jay screamed and ran forward. Hoyt stood there, grinning, holding the axe from the shed in his left hand. He didn't raise it to defend himself. He simply waited and let the guard overtake him. A second later, Jay was on top of him, punching, tearing, strangling the life from him.

"I'll kill you!" Jay screamed shrilly. "I'll kill you, you son of a bitch!"

"You can't," said Hoyt with that smile. "Can't kill me."

"Damn... sick... bastard..." Fingers tightening, burrowing into flesh, seeking death and justice.

"You can't." Hoyt's face was as purple as a bruise, his eyes bulging, his mouth grinning. "Can't kill me... can never kill me."

Jay screamed hysterically. Continued to strangle until his hands ached, then grew numb.

"Never," the inmate told him, calmly, serenely. "Never can kill me."

It was John Masterson's first morning on the job. His superior, Fred Garcia, was giving him a tour of Floor Three when the screaming started.

"I'll kill you! I'll kill you, you son of a bitch!"

"Who the hell is that?" he asked, startled. He breathed deeply, trying to calm himself. He didn't want his new boss to get the idea that he was a man who was easy to rattle.

"Oh, that's inmate number 17," Fred told him. He seemed unconcerned, as though he had heard this type of thing a hundred times before.

"Damn... sick... bastard..."

Garcia sensed the new employee's unease. "Come on. We'll check on him."

Halfway down the corridor, John thought he heard another voice. Strangely calm and serene. "Never. Never can kill me."

"What's going on?" he had to ask.

They reached the door of Number 17 and peered through the little, reinforced glass window. A tall, lanky man was getting up off the floor and walking to the wall next to his bunk. There was a uniform hanging on a peg on the wall. He whistled cheerfully as he began to remove his orange coveralls.

"His name is Jay Wilmore," Garcia explained. "He was a former prison guard here. A good, dependable man for five years on the job. Then one morning, he clocked out, drove home, and killed his wife and daughter with an axe. A horrible thing… him ending up back here after committing such an unthinkable crime as that."

Confused, John watched through the window as Wilmore finished undressing and then began to dress in the guard uniform hanging from the peg. "I… I don't understand. Why do you let…?"

"Let him pretend?" The chief guard smiled sadly. "It pacifies him… keeps him manageable. He's got a whole routine mapped out in his head. Dressing for work, clocking in, walking around his cell all day, like he's making his rounds. He even has a cast of characters to keep him company. A chief guard—like me—named Prater, fellow guards named Ted and Henry, and even a warden named Thompson. He has them all worked out in that warped brain of his—their life stories, wives and children, what they eat for lunch, when they go to the restroom."

"Weird," said John. He watched as Jay Wilmore finished dressing and taking a timecard from under his pillow, walked over the wall and said "Cla-click". Then he returned the card to his bunk and began to walk back and forth across the eight-by-ten area of his cell.

"It was terrible what he did…how he snapped like that for no reason at all," Fred told him. "But he's pretty much harmless now. He'll walk around like that for eight hours, clock out at the end of his shift, put on his coveralls, and be an inmate again. It's been going like that for five years now, just like clockwork."

I guess you're just going to have to get accustomed to it, John told himself. *All the wackos and the little games they play.*

"Come on," Garcia told him. "Let's go to the conference room and we'll do your orientation. I'll get us some coffee. How do you like yours?"

"Black," John said absently. "No cream, no sugar."

They were halfway down the corridor when laughter echoed behind them.

John Masterson looked around to see the face of Jay Wilmore plastered against the glass, staring at him through the little window. His smile was broad and seemed to reach from ear to ear… his eyes bright and shiny, looking like someone in the throes of a high fever.

The murderer gave him a knowing wink. For some reason, it sent a shiver down the guard's spine.

"Hey, new guy… let's talk."

YEA, THOUGH I DRIVE

There was a massacre in progress on I-75.

The interstate system stretched from Florida, across Georgia and Tennessee, clear to northern Kentucky. Until the autumn of that year, it was known mainly for its scenic beauty and the Southern hospitality exhibited at the restaurants and motels that served as overnight havens between the long miles of rural solitude.

Then the killings began.

In three short months, the "Roadside Butcher" had murdered eighteen travelers along Interstate 75, each one varying in degree of brutality and mutilation. Some drivers were found sitting in their cars or eighteen-wheelers with their throats neatly slashed from ear to ear. Others were found lying at the side of the road, sliced open from gullet to groin, gutted like a deer at hunting season. And then there were the more grisly of the Butcher's victims… those who had been hacked to death, dismembered, or decapitated. The strange thing about the whole ordeal was that there was no definite pattern. The victims had been hitchhikers and drifters, as well as vacationing travelers and burly truckers who regularly frequented the eight-hundred-and-fifty-mile stretch of southern interstate.

The Highway Patrol was out in full force, as were the FBI, but the increase in law enforcement didn't seem to deter the Butcher from performing his fiendish whims. It got so that veteran travelers of the road began to carry pistols and sawed-off shotguns, secretly stashed in glove compartments and sleeper cabs. Most of the truck stops began to sell a popular bumper sticker which read "YEA, THOUGH I DRIVE ALONG THE HIGHWAY OF THE SHADOW OF DEATH, I WILL FEAR NO EVIL, FOR I AM THE MEANEST S.O.B. ALIVE ON I-75!" However, at least a couple of those fearless motorists were found lying across their front seats with their throats cut down to the neckbone or their entrails dangling from the rearview mirror like strands of Christmas garland.

The sudden increase in freeway paranoia did not help Mark Casey's situation any. He had been a drifter for years, possessing a nagging desire for wandering and the freedom of the open road. Before the chaos on I-75, the long hair and beard had not hampered his ability to catch a ride, either from one exit to the next, or straight through to his intended destination. But these days, hitchhiking was becoming one big pain in the ass. Whenever he hung out at a truck stop or stood at the roadside with his thumb in the air, he felt the eyes of potential rides appraising him negatively and noticing his uncanny resemblance to Charles Manson. Never mind that the wild eyes and swastika carved on the forehead was absent, the motorist would still see all that hair and the baggy field jacket that could easily conceal any number of sharp implements. They would see all that in one fleeting glance, shake their heads "fat chance", and drive on, leaving Mark frustrated, sore-footed, and cold.

If it hadn't been for his sudden pairing with Clifford Lee Gates, Mark was sure he would have ended walking clear from Florida to Ohio that week in mid-December. Clifford Lee was a lanky boy of eighteen from Cloverfield, Georgia, a farming community that boasted a gas station, a general store, and a whopping census of one hundred and eighty-two citizens. Clifford Lee had high aspirations of becoming a country music singer. His constantly good-natured grin and overabundance of optimism were signs that he actually believed that he would make it big in Nashville, armed only with a beat-up Fender acoustic and his rural charm, despite his obvious lack of money and connections. Mark knew at once, upon meeting him at a greasy spoon called Lou's Place, that he should watch out for this wide-eyed innocent. The boy would be easy pickings with a psychopath like the Butcher on the loose.

Anyway, it was Clifford Lee's infectious charm that netted them a ride north with an overweight copier salesman by the name of A.J. Rudman. Rudman was returning home to Louisville from a Xerox convention held in Orlando the previous week. They had overheard him talking to the truck stop waitress and, when he was paying his check at the register, Clifford Lee approached him with a big ole country-bumpkin grin. The middle-aged salesman was apprehensive at first, eyeing the young man's bearded friend with immediate suspicion. But soon, the boy's benevolence won over the man's worries and he told them he would give them a lift that stormy winter night.

The long drive started out in silence, a silence born of tension and uneasiness. Mark sat in the front, while Clifford Lee took the back seat, upon Rudman's insistence. Obviously, the Kentucky salesman wanted the more suspicious of the two where he could keep an eye on him.

Mark suffered the blatant mistrust quietly, just thankful that he and the Georgia farmboy were inside a warm, dry car and not humping the dark countryside in the pouring rain.

By the time they had crossed the state of Georgia and were a few miles into Tennessee, the mood had lightened somewhat. Idle conversation had echoed between the three and Clifford had even picked some country tunes on his guitar. The hillbilly twang in Gates's voice grated on Mark's nerves, but he settled into the Lincoln's plush velour seat and tried to enjoy it anyway. A.J. Rudman seemed to be having digestive problems. He drove with one hand on the wheel and the other tucked into the midsection of his tan raincoat over his prominent beer belly. *Probably has a bad peptic ulcer,* thought Mark, not without a flare of mean-spirited satisfaction. *I guess that's what you get when you're a part of the corporate rat race these days, right, Pops?*

"Where are you boys bound for?" Rudman asked out of pure boredom. His nervousness seemed to be gradually increasing for some reason. He was popping Tums like they were jellybeans.

"Well, I'm heading for Dayton," Mark replied, trying to inject a friendly tone in hopes of dispelling the man's distrust in him. "I'm going home to my parents' place for Christmas. Mom always has a big spread laid out—turkey, candied yams, the works."

"How about you, son?" the salesman asked over his shoulder.

Clifford Lee looked up from his guitar and grinned sheepishly. "I'm off to Nashville, Tennessee, to be a big country star. I grew up on country and western music. Me and my pa, we'd listen to the Grand Ole Opry every Saturday night. I got to singing and picking on the guitar here and the folks said, 'Why, you're as good as any of 'em, Clifford Lee! You oughta head on up to Music City and try your luck.' So that's what I aim to do."

During the farmboy's long-winded explanation, Mark noticed his hand squeeze past the guitar strings and disappear into the hole of the Fender's hourglass body. He grinned. Surely Clifford Lee didn't have a secret stash hidden inside his guitar. Mark had been around enough potheads to know a few who hid their grass in strange places, including musical instruments. But, no, Clifford Lee Gates was no more a smoker of marijuana than Snoop Dog was the Imperial Wizard of the Ku Klux Klan.

Still, the thought of a good smoke, straight or otherwise, brought out that craving for nicotine in Mark Casey. Since Rudman seemed to be smoker himself, Mark absently reached into an inside pocket of his olive drab coat for a pack of Marlboros, figuring the guy wouldn't mind if he indulged. Suddenly, the big Lincoln Continental was whipping back and forth across the double lanes of the northbound stretch of I-75, shooting onto the paved shoulder on the far side and braking to such a sharp and screeching halt that the bearded hitchhiker would have butted his head against the windshield if his seatbelt hadn't been buckled.

A breathless silence hung within the car for a long moment. The pattering of steady rainfall on the roof was the only sound to be heard. Then Mark turned and regarded the pale-faced businessman. "What the hell did you do that for?" he yelled. "Are you trying to kill us or something?"

A.J. Rudman swallowed dryly, his right hand still pressed against his gastric woes. "What were *you* doing?" he croaked back. "What were you reaching for… inside your coat?"

"My smokes, man, that's all!" Mark pulled the cigarettes from his pocket and slammed them down on the dashboard. He stared at the businessman incredulously. "You thought I was going for a knife, didn't you? You thought that I was the freaking Roadside Butcher! That I was gonna pull a big knife outta my coat and carve your sonofabitching head clean off. That's exactly what you thought, wasn't it?" He snorted and shook his head in disgust. "Well, I ain't the damned Butcher… you got that? I may look like some drug-crazed devil worshiper to you, but I'm just a regular guy trying to get from point A to point B and, believe it or not, I'm just as jumpy as you are where that butchering crazy is concerned."

"Well, I thought…" began Rudman in embarrassment. "It's just that you reached into your pocket without any warning and…"

"Yeah… yeah, I know, man. Just a big misunderstanding. Why don't you just loosen up and put us back on the road again, okay?"

The salesman nodded. He was about to shift back into drive, when Clifford Lee chuckled from the back seat. "Shucks, Mr. Rudman, ol' Mark ain't the killer. Shoot fire, he's one of the nicest fellas I've ever met," he said with a grin. "Heck, naw, he ain't the Roadside Butcher. But you want to know something kinda funny? I *am*!" And, with that, the farmboy reached around the padded headrest and laid a pearl-handled straight razor against A.J. Rudman's flabby throat.

"What are you doing, man?" Mark asked. He looked at the goofy Georgian with the cowlicked crop of reddish-blond hair and the slightly bucked teeth. Suddenly, as he stared into that freckled face, he realized that what he had initially interpreted as down-home naiveté had actually been a dark, underlying madness all along.

"What do you think I'm a-doing?" giggled Clifford Lee. The honed edge of the shaving razor glinted sinisterly in the pale glow of the dashboard light. "I'm fixing to kill this nice gentleman. Now, don't go looking so danged surprised, Mark. And don't worry... I ain't gonna hurt you none. You're my friend."

Mark Casey watched in numb disbelief as Clifford Lee made his victim shut off the engine, unbuckle his seat belt and, ever so carefully, climb out into the stormy night. As if in a trance, Mark left the car as well, walking around the rear bumper to watch the inevitable bloodletting. Clifford had Rudman's head pulled back by the hair, the straight razor positioned at a deadly angle above the man's carotid artery.

"But *why*, man?" asked Mark, his stomach sinking at the dread of having to stand there and watch a crimson gorge open beneath Rudman's double chin. "Why are you doing this?"

Clifford Lee Gates gave his road mate a toothy grin and shrugged. "Why not?"

Then something very strange happened. Something that neither Mark nor Clifford anticipated. A.J. Rudman still had his hand tucked inside his raincoat. It had been there all during the tedious transition from dry car to wet pavement. Mark had just figured the poor guy's ulcer was about to explode. But he saw now that hadn't been the case.

Rudman slowly withdrew his hand and—clutched in his pudgy fingers—was the biggest damned bowie knife that Mark Casey had ever seen in his life.

He didn't know exactly why he did it, but he yelled "Look out, Clifford!" The razor-wielding musician leaped back just as Rudman turned and slashed in a broad arc that would have taken out most of the boy's abdomen if he had been standing in the same spot. The twelve-inch blade sliced through the cold misty air with a loud *swoosh*.

Rudman laughed. "The Butcher like hell! You're nothing but a damned copycat... and not a very good one at that. Oh, slitting throats is just fine and dandy, but it shows a great lack of creativity."

The middle-aged salesman passed the heavy knife teasingly from one hand to the other. "Come on, farmboy, let me show you how I express myself."

Mark could only stand and watch as the two men squared off in the twin beams of the Lincoln's headlights. The guitar-picker stood poised and ready, the joint of the razor's blade and handle gripped between thumb and forefinger. The salesman crouched in a classic fighter's stance, the big bowie held, long and perfectly balanced, in one chubby hand. Like a couple of duelists, they circled one another, appraising strengths and weaknesses. Then they came together in a violent fury of flashing steel and spurting blood.

Mark knew he should have run for his life, but he was transfixed. Grunts of pain and the ripping of clothing and flesh echoed across the empty lanes of Interstate 75. The frightened hitchhiker witnessed the awful blood feud, torn between revulsion and fascination. He rooted for neither man, although one had been a newfound friend until only a few moments ago.

The fight ended abruptly when the two men struggled to the pavement and rolled toward the front of the car, away from Mark's view. A torturous scream split the air, followed by a wet gurgle. For a moment, the headlights revealed only the glistening pavement ahead and the driving rainfall. Then a single form stood up.

"I won," grinned Clifford Lee.

Mark backed away as the young man started around the car for him. Clifford's denim jacket was in bloody tatters, his face crisscrossed with deep gashes. He had traded his razor for the broad-bladed bowie. "You know when I said I wouldn't hurt you, Mark?" asked Clifford Lee brushing aside a flap of loose skin that hung above his left eye. "Well, hell, I lied. I'm sorry, buddy, but I'm gonna have to kill you, too. Can't leave no loose ends, you know. Hope you understand."

But Mark didn't understand. He leaped off the road and into the darkness.

With a maniacal cackle, Clifford Lee was in hot pursuit. Unfortunately, there was no solid ground beyond the glow of the car's high beams, only a steep drop-off into a wooded hollow below. The two tumbled head over heels, landing at the bottom of the grassy incline. Mark was the first one up and that was to his advantage. Clifford Lee was groggy from bashing his head against a rock on the way down. He crawled toward his lost blade, but didn't quite make it. Mark reached the big knife first and, without a second's hesitation, drove it between his traveling buddy's heaving shoulder blades.

"What'd you do that for?" croaked Clifford Lee, blood spraying from his mouth and nostrils. "I thought we were pals."

"I thought so, too," replied Mark. "God help me, I really did." He withdrew the knife and buried it to the hilt one more time, just to be on the safe side.

Moments later, Mark was climbing back up the grassy face of the hollow for the interstate. His wild high of exhilaration and relief faded into confusion when he reached the lip of the thoroughfare. A dark form crouched beside the bloody body of A.J. Rudman, then stood and shucked a revolver from a side holster when he saw Mark stumble out of the darkness.

"Killed him..." Mark managed, trying to explain, pointing back into the hollow. "I killed him... stabbed him..."

The state trooper lifted his .357 Magnum in a two-handed hold. "You just stop right there," he barked. "Drop it and don't move a muscle."

Mark couldn't understand why the lawman refused to listen. "The Butcher..." he gasped. "Dead... I killed the..."

"I said, *drop the knife!* This is my last warning!"

"But you don't understand..." Mark sputtered. He lifted his hands to reason with the man and there it was, the bowie knife, completely forgotten until it flashed electric blue in the patrol car's cascading lights.

Three shots rang out. Three hollow point slugs obliterated the top of Mark Casey's skull and sent his body sprawling across the white borderline of the medium. Clumps of brain and splinters of skull littered the dark pavement, but they were soon washed away as the black rains of the storm-soaked Interstate 75 and scrubbed it clean.

Officer Hal Olsen holstered his revolver and walked back to the patrol car. He sat down heavily and picked up the mike of his radio. "Unit H-108 to headquarters. Send me additional backup, will you? I've got one hell of a mess out here on 75, two miles north of the third Chattanooga exit. I've just shot the Roadside Butcher, but not before he killed two others." When he was assured that help was on its way, the officer replaced the mike and turned his radio off.

He sat there and stared at the body clad in an Army fatigue jacket and faded jeans. Shaking his head, he withdrew an object wrapped in canvas from beneath his car seat and walked over to where Mark Casey laid.

"I don't know who you were, fella, but you just got me off the hook."

Officer Olsen withdrew a long-bladed machete from the wrapping and hefted it's comforting weight in his hand one last time, before tossing it as far as he could into the wet darkness of the backwoods hollow. Then he returned to the car and waited for his fellow officers to arrive.

SUMMER OF THE THUMB

Sometimes people ask about it. My right thumb... or the lack of one. I'm a carpenter by trade, so they figure that's what did it. I cut it off with a SKIL saw or some other power tool. I don't say yes or no. I try to make the answer as vague as possible. It's none of their damn business anyway.

I just shove my hand in my pocket and tell them it happened in '82 and leave it that. Folks who live around here... well, they know. But they're polite enough not to bring it up.

About why the thumb is gone.

About what happened that summer.

A freckle-faced, blonde-haired girl named Trish Crowe was my best friend that summer. We had attended Pikesville Elementary together since kindergarten. We hated each other's guts at the beginning, when we were five. She was prissy and snotty, and I was insufferably obnoxious. But, later on, we sort of grew on each other. By the time we were ten we were nearly inseparable. I remember when Tommy McFee picked on me after school, claimed she was my girlfriend, made those kissy sounds and told us to "get a room". My ears had turned blood red in embarrassment. And Trish had walked over with a sweet and friendly smile and nailed him square in the nuts. Tommy had puked his guts up and Trish and I looked at one another and I knew right then and there she would always be there for me.

In the summer of 1982, we were twelve. Gangly and awkward.

Pimples speckling her face and my voice unable to determine whether it wanted to be high or low. But we didn't pay attention to that. There was crazy shit going on around town, so we had more serious things to think about than our own freakishly evolving bodies.

Someone was taking children. The youngest had been six, the oldest fourteen. Boys and girls. Kids out riding their bikes or walking home from the store. By the end of June, there had been seven. Some had been found and some hadn't. Those that showed up were discovered in ditches or in the woods. Dead. Their funerals had been sadder than Grandma dying of cancer or Uncle Hugh from a coronary. The caskets were closed and stayed closed. Only the police and the families knew why. Whatever had happened to those kids, it hadn't left them pretty enough to lie on satin pillows, basking openly in the muted glow of the visitation chapel of Brewer's Funeral Home.

Trish and I talked about it a lot that June. Trying to figure out who had taken them or exactly what he—or she—had done to them. There were rumors around town that they had been: A) dismembered, B) decapitated, and C) skinned alive. If that was the case, it would explain the closed caskets and the pale, hollow-eyed faces of their parents. Faces, like ghost skulls, that hovered around town for weeks—and years—afterward.

Our parents told us to be extra careful. To not talk to strangers and to report anyone hanging around that we didn't know. Trish said it was probably someone we *did* know. Maybe a garage mechanic or a grocery store clerk or even someone we went to church with. She said her mom read those true crime paperbacks you buy at the drugstore and that the mass murderers and serial killers on the covers didn't look like monsters at all. They looked like regular moms and dads, like the police officer that lived across the street or the janitor at the high school.

That wasn't all that we dwelled on, though. I was obsessed with horror movies and so was she. The Stardust Theater downtown showed movies like *Annie, E.T.,* and *Fast Times at Ridgemont High,* but they showed the scary movies, too. So far that year, we had gone to see *Poltergeist, Basket Case,* and *The Beast Within.* Movies that we probably had no business watching at that age. But Trish's brother, Brody, swept up the theatre between shows and he'd let us in the EXIT door when no one was looking. I think he did it because Trish had something on him; maybe she caught him smoking or he had a *Hustler* or *Playboy* hidden under his mattress.

Yeah, we sure loved those horror movies.

And that's what got us into trouble. That's what led to the thumb.

Around the fourth week in June, I had it in my head that I wanted to see *The Thing*. I had seen the photos in *Fangoria*—the twisted and mutated flesh, the upside-down head with the spider legs, and Kurt Russell's bodacious beard encrusted with ice. Trish wasn't a hundred percent on board, though.

"It's too weird," she said, wrinkling that cute, freckled nose of hers.

"Freaky!"

"It's Carpenter," I told her. "It's supposed to be freaky."

"I don't know if we should. It has, you know, the *F-word*."

"How do you know?" I wanted to say the word out loud, but I didn't... because you never knew when a Sunday school teacher or one of your parents' friends might be within earshot.

"Cause Brody told me," she said, "and that's his favorite word ever... when Mom and Dad aren't around."

"It can't be any worse than *The Evil Dead* or *American Werewolf in London*. We saw those last year when we were eleven and you were fine."

Trish had shuddered. "But all that blood and mangled flesh and *alien* stuff!"

But eventually, I talked her into it. And we agreed to sneak out of our houses on the weekend of the twenty-fifth and meet behind the Stardust, then wait in the dark next to the fire exit until Brody let us in.

But, as it turned out, we weren't the only ones lurking in the night.

We got there fifteen minutes before the nine o'clock show. It was hot and muggy. Lightning bugs winked on and off in the vacant lot behind the building, and crickets sang in the high weeds. I sensed Trish standing beside me, really close, and smelled her summer sweat and the scent of Herbal Essences shampoo in her hair. I had an urge to reach out and touch her, or hold her hand, or—*Jesus*—even kiss her. But I fought the urge. I couldn't see her, but I heard her sigh and wondered if she had expected me to do something and was disappointed that I hadn't.

Inside, we heard the music for the ending credits and knew we had about seven or eight more minutes to wait. That's when someone came out of the night and grabbed Trish from behind.

It had been cloudy that night, cloudy enough to cover a half-moon. About the time that Trish had gasped, those clouds moved, and I saw a man's hands. One was clamped on top of Trish's head, while another pressed a handkerchief to her nose and mouth. There was a strong medicinal smell, like a doctor's office.

I watched, frozen, as Trish struggled. Then her eyes rolled up into her head and she grew limp.

"Come along, boy," said a voice. It was said in a whisper, but it sounded familiar, one I'd heard before. Maybe more than once.

I took a step or two backward, like I was going to turn and run. But that was impossible. I was never going to leave Trish. Even if it meant getting my head cut off or every inch of skin flayed from my body.

"Come with me," he said, a little sharper than before. "You run and I'll keep this pressed against her nose until she dies." I could see teeth in the moonlight. They were shiny and cruel. "Believe me, if she breaths enough it, she will."

So, I went. He lifted Trish into his arms, and I followed him to the cab of a pickup truck. My heart skipped a beat when I saw it. I immediately knew who it belonged to.

He laid Trish across the front seat, and I climbed in next to her. Then he slammed the door and drove us away. He didn't drive very far. Three or four blocks from the center of town at the very most.

Time has a way of distorting when you're scared half to death. Minutes feel like hours and hours feel like years. At the time—after the abduction—we had no idea how long we were there. Later on, we found out it was only four days.

He put us in a storm cellar. Some of the older homes in town had them because of a nasty rash of tornados that almost destroyed Pikesville in the late 1950s. Heavy double doors were all that could be seen from above ground. Beyond them were concrete steps leading down to a dark pit. The place was dank and smelled of mildew and mold. And other, nastier things. There was a single bulb hanging from the ceiling, probably no more than a forty-watt. It looked like someone had splashed the concrete walls with rusty brown paint. But it wasn't.

Mr. Spencer didn't try to hide his identity. He didn't seem to care. Our eighth-grade science teacher—the one who taught us about the solar system and the Periodic Table of Elements and how to dissect an earthworm—had no qualms whatsoever about us seeing his face or knowing who he was. I remember feeling frightened and sick to my stomach... because I knew it didn't matter. And that we wouldn't be leaving until he was finished with us... and we were dumped in a ditch... or lying in a coffin with the lid closed and locked.

He took our clothes and left us with only our underwear, me in my white Fruit of the Looms and Trish in her undershirt and panties. We watched, stunned, as he neatly placed our clothes on hangers and hung them from a ventilation pipe overhead. They joined seven other sets of clothes of varying sizes and genders.

Mr. Spencer didn't tie us up or chain us to the wall. He let us roam free. But he stuck strips of silver duct tape over our mouths, so none of his neighbors would hear us scream. He warned that if we took them off, he would sew our lips together with needle and thread. In science class, we had once witnessed him sew a bullfrog's belly back up after he had opened its torso with a scalpel to show us its beating heart. So, we knew he possessed the skill to do exactly what he said.

After he left, we mostly just crouched in the corners and cried.

Trish cried the hardest. Several times I almost went over and held her. But we were both almost naked and I was afraid it would scare her even more.

Mr. Spencer brought us food. Lots of food.

Hamburgers and fries and corndogs and chicken nuggets from McDonald's and the Dairy Queen down the street. He would remove the duct tape with a yank. A cruel gleam in his eyes told us that he knew it hurt like hell and he didn't care. We weren't hungry, but he stood over us until we ate every bite, then he would put fresh tape back on. I remembered a fairy tale my mom once read from a Little Golden Book. The witch fattening up Hansel and Gretel for the oven.

When we were alone, Trish would lay curled into a ball and talk to herself. "He's going to kill us... kill us... kill us." I tried to lift her spirits, but there were none there to be lifted.

I took to walking around the shelter; searching, studying. There were bottled water and food packets on wooden shelves on the walls, the kind you could buy at the Army Surplus store in Memphis. Sometimes I would mount the concrete steps and push on the wooden doors. They didn't budge. He had secured them shut with a big Yale padlock that a jackhammer couldn't damage. Through the cracks in the boards I could see sunlight in the daytime and moonlight at night.

I eventually found an old screwdriver on one of the shelves and began to pry at the metal beyond the gap between the two doors. But it was no use. We weren't going anywhere.

Trish would watch me from her corner. Small and dirty, smelling of urine.

Resigned to the fact that we would never ride our bikes again. Or sleep in soft beds. Or be gently tucked in and kissed goodnight.

"We're gonna die, you know." Her voice was flat... like she wasn't scared at all. But she was. She was terrified.

And so was I.

Then it happened… after what seemed an eternity. But it was only the fourth day, on a Wednesday.

A smell began to filter in from the outside. My dad had grilled out enough that I knew the acrid scent of charcoal briquettes and lighter fluid when I smelled it. The odor was hot and final and like roasted death.

Then we heard him outside. Getting things ready. Unfolding the sort of camp table you bought down at the hardware store. The jingle of silverware as he hummed a Journey song both Trish and I had heard a bazillion times on the radio that summer. Then there was the rattle of the padlock, a crisp *click* as a key released the clasp, and the squeal of unoiled hinges.

As sunlight flooded the shelter, I pulled Trish to her feet. She didn't want to budge from her spot on the floor at first, but suddenly both of us knew this was it. This was the *moment*.

Startled, I looked around. Mr. Spencer was on the concrete steps. Naked, wearing only a chef's hat and a long white apron that read LICENSE TO GRILL. It would have been funny, maybe even hilarious, if he hadn't been holding a meat cleaver in one hand and a butcher knife in the other.

Trish tried to scream, but her terror only sounded muffled and defeated beneath the tape. I ran toward our captor, maybe to protect my friend, maybe to try to slip past him and make it to freedom. It was just a reaction out of panic… there was no bravery to the act at all, not like Stallone in *First Blood* or Schwarzenegger in *Conan the Barbarian*. Just a frightened little boy trying to delay the inevitable.

Mr. Spencer lashed out with a foot and kicked me backward. I stumbled and hit a support post hard enough to drive the breath from my lungs. I reached out with a hand to steady myself with the post and something whistled past my ear and there was a noise. A *thunk*. Hot liquid squirted into my face, my eyes, my mouth. I moaned and saw that my hand was missing a piece. There was no pain at first. Just a numbed feeling, like when the dentist pricks your gums before filling or pulling a tooth.

I looked away from my bleeding hand and watched, almost amazed, as Mr. Spencer stooped down and found my thumb. He stared at it, as though mesmerized. Put it in his mouth and bit down. Began to chew flesh and splinter bone. He grinned—the cracks between his teeth wet and red—as he stepped forward and raised the cleaver to bring it down upon my head.

Then Trish regained her composure for one clear second and pulled a Tommy McFee on him. She reared back and punched him in the balls as hard as she possibly could.

Mr. Spencer seemed to forget us then. A funny expression crossed his face, which grew increasingly red, then purple. He sank to his knees and gurgled. His eyes bulged. The thing he had been eating had lodged in his throat.

He was choking on my thumb.

I grabbed Trish's hand with my only good one and we were gone. Up the steps, through the open doors of the storm cellar... and we were free.

We ran across the patio, past the Weber grill, and around the side of Mr. Spencer's house. Down the gravel drive where the mail carrier, Mrs. Johnson, was putting an electric bill and a copy of the *Sports Illustrated Swimsuit Edition* in our teacher's mailbox.

I'm fifty-two now. Got a wife and two grown daughters. One is a nurse, and the other is graduating high school this year. We live in the house I grew up in. I got it after Mom died. Dad passed away in 2012 of prostate cancer.

My wife didn't understand my reasoning at first, about why I wanted to see *him* again. Why I wanted to dredge up all those horrible memories and confront him, face to face. Maybe I really didn't know myself. Maybe I left a piece of myself—besides my thumb—back in that storm cellar. Something I needed to find and take back.

I've been petitioning for a meeting for three years. Writing the corrections board, state senators, even the governor. They don't want me to see the Mad Scientist (those stupid newscasters and their labels!). They don't think I have a right to see him, even if I was one of the only two victims that escaped. After all, he did kill and devour eighteen children. Seven in Pikesville, three in Memphis, and eight in other states in the South and Midwest.

But my tenacity won out and I finally got my chance. It would be a virtual meeting—my choice of Zoom or Skype—but at least I would be able to see him, and he would see me.

I remember how agitated I was the hour before the scheduled time.

"You can call it off," she said, hopefully.

"You know I can't," I told her.

"Stubborn." But she smiled and nodded.

My youngest daughter set up her Chromebook on the kitchen table and kissed me on the forehead. Then she and her mother went out. Where to I had no idea. Maybe to Dairy Queen for ice cream. To give me my time... with him.

My heart pounded as words on the screen read "Wait for your host to begin your session". Then the screen opened and there he was. Old and weathered, but recognizable. Same Army crewcut. Same black horn-rimmed glasses. Dressed in gray coveralls, his liver-spotted wrists handcuffed. I imagined shackles on his ankles as well.

We regarded one another. He had a blank expression on his face at first. Then he leaned in, puzzled. "I know you. Don't I know you?"

I said nothing. Just lifted my right hand.

He grinned. His teeth were yellowed from smoking. There was no longer blood within the gaps.

"Yes," he said softly. Eyes twinkling behind the lenses. "I know you. The one who got away."

We stared at one another for a long moment. "I just wanted to see you again," I told him. *And let you know I'm not afraid of you anymore*, I wanted to say, but I didn't.

"Why? Did you miss me? Miss the storm cellar? Miss seeing your little bitch in her frilly little panties?"

I knew what he was doing. Playing with me, baiting me. Trying to set off a fuse. I didn't give in. "I'm not afraid of you, Mr. Spencer," I finally got up the nerve to say. It sounded oddly flat and emotionless in my ears. Decades away I heard Trish say *We're gonna die, you know.*

Spencer laughed. "Are you sure? Aren't you just the least bit afraid?" His eyes searched mine. Looking for cracks. Trying to get in. "Remember the stains on the walls? The food to fatten? The grill, hot and ready?"

My heart pounded harder. A pulse throbbed in my temple. I felt lightheaded. *God… don't let me faint in front of him.*

The old man leaned forward until his face filled the screen entirely. "And you know what?"

I fought to remain silent. But I wanted to know. So, I answered. "What?"

His smile was predatory, the tongue between his teeth glistening. "I can still *taste* you."

I wanted to react. I wanted to glare and cuss at him. But I couldn't. I couldn't speak. I couldn't breathe. I was twelve again.

Then, mercifully, the uniformed arm of a prison guard reached over Mr. Spencer's stooped shoulder and ended the session.

That night, I tossed and turned. Couldn't sleep.

Smelled the dankness of mildew and mold. Saw the darkness of stains on the wall.

Trish reached out and took my right hand. Cradled four fingers. Lightly caressed the place where the thumb should have been.

She said my name softly. It had never sounded sweeter on her lips.

"You were right," I whispered hoarsely. "I should have listened."

"Hush. It's over now."

I nodded. For her sake more than mine.

In the darkness, I still saw his face, hollowed by age.

The grin, hungry and sly.

And, beyond Trish's pleasant smell, the stench of carrion breath.

WOODSHED

Number 38 was nearly to the end of its afternoon route, with only two more stops to go.

Cole Brenner sat in one of the middle seats that day, not in the very back the way he usually did. The school bus was one of Mangrum County's newest and longest at thirty-four feet and accommodating 72 passengers. At that moment, there were only three people in the vehicle: Cole, Billy McDonald, and the driver, Miss Anderson.

"Here you go, Billy," Miss Anderson called out. The big Bluebird's air brakes hissed, and everyone shifted forward on their seats as the bus slowed, then came to a gradual halt. Miss Anderson pulled the lever near the dashboard, and the flashing STOP sign and folding doors engaged at the same time.

Billy, one of Mangrum County High's "nerdy" students, adjusted his backpack, gathered an armload of textbooks (Sociology, Calculus, Physics), and started down the narrow aisle between the seats. Cole grinned and eased his foot out, intending to trip the boy, but Miss Anderson's eyes glared at him in the extra-wide rearview mirror.

"Don't you *dare*, Mr. Brenner!" she warned. Her voice attempted to sound gruff and authoritative, but Cole heard what lay beneath. Weakness and uncertainty. And, hopefully, fear.

Cole grinned slyly and reluctantly pulled his foot back. Billy passed by, afraid to even look at the bully. Just acknowledging that he was there might draw a wrath much worse than the playful tripping. It was bound to happen, tomorrow or the next day, either in the privacy of the boys' restroom or in gym class when it was dodgeball day.

"Bye, Billy," the driver said sweetly. "Have a good evening."

Billy McDonald's ears reddened the way they always did whenever a female talked to him. "Bye, Miss Anderson. You, too."

Then the boy was down the steep steps, off the bus, and shuffling across the lawn to his house. The lever was pulled, the door closed, and the bus lurched into life again, carrying them toward their next stop, Cole's house ... a half mile further on Newsome Branch Road.

As the bus rumbled along, Cole sat perfectly still and stared at the back of the driver's head. He hated Miss Anderson. Hated the woman's guts with a passion. The only interaction he had ever had with her had been negative. *"Mr. Brenner, quiet down!", "Mr. Brenner, leave him/her alone!", "Mr. Brenner, I DO NOT want to hear that sort of language on my bus!"* She had been his bus driver since the sixth grade, and not once had she had a single pleasant thing to say to him. Of course, he had never given her any reason to. Cole was a first-rate asshole and bully, and he knew it. Cruelty and intimidation were what made him tick.

Yes, Cole despised her, even more than the principal or the teachers at school. Even more than his parents, if that was possible. But he *wanted* her. Not just sexually, but for other desires as well. Darker desires. He had grown weary of the occasional cat or dog. They could scream, but they had no words to feed him. He craved a diet of pleading and begging, crying desperately for a mercy that he was unwilling to provide—or incapable of providing.

As the bus continued down the country road, Cole considered all that he knew about Tina Anderson. She was plain as an old dishrag: light brown hair, thick-lensed eyeglasses, and a narrow face with a sharp nose and weak chin. Her body wasn't bad. Nice boobs and a round ass ... but then, he was seventeen, so he could have very well looked at a hollow log in the woods and gotten horny. Miss Anderson was known in the community as quiet and introverted. She wasn't married. She went to church ... even taught a Sunday school class, or so he had heard. He didn't know it firsthand. Cole had never stepped foot in a church in his life.

He also knew she lived at the dead end of Newsome Branch Road, a good mile or two in the woods past his house. Way out there in the middle of nowhere, all alone ... where no one could hear her scream. If anyone gave her a reason to.

Cole grinned to himself. His pulse quickened as he dug something out of his jeans pocket. The steel of the folding knife was cool in his hand. He snapped it open with a flick of his wrist, just the way his father had taught him. Of course, Dad would have never shown him that trick if he had known his son's true intentions.

He looked down at the blade, hidden from view behind the seat in front of him. It was five inches long and sharp as a razor. He knew that well because he had spent hours honing it on a whetstone from his father's workshop. Just raking the edge of the steel back and forth, back and forth ... thinking about Miss Anderson.

They were a quarter of a mile from his house now. He took a deep breath and stood up, one hand on the top of the neighboring seat to steady himself, the other grasping the folding hunter.

"Take your seat, Mr. Brenner!" Miss Anderson's voice was high-pitched and nasally, annoying and grating in the teenager's ears. "You are not to stand until the bus comes to a complete stop."

He ignored her demand for obedience and kept on coming. He held the knife behind his right thigh so she wouldn't see it. Not until just the right moment.

"Do I need to stop this bus, young man?"

Cole continued up the center aisle between the empty seats. Slowly, methodically. Grinning that greasy, smart-ass grin of his.

"Mr. Brenner ... do you want me to call your parents?" she asked. She held her cell phone in view as if to fortify her threat. Her voice had a different tone to it now. An edge. Of panic? Fear? "I will, you know. I've done it before."

Cole was almost there. *You ain't calling nobody,* he thought. *Maybe on your God ... for help ... but he's not going to hear you. Not way out there in those woods. It'll be just you and me.*

He looked through the windshield. The mailbox next to his driveway grew nearer and nearer. Before she could apply the brakes, he sat down in the seat behind her, reached around, and laid the flat of the knife against her throat. It startled her so much that she lost hold of her phone. It tumbled from her hand, bounced across the floorboard, and clattered into the stairwell of the double folding doors.

"Keep going," he said. For emphasis, he grabbed the hair on the back of her head and gave it a painful tug backward.

He could see her eyes in the rearview mirror. They were big and surprised, like a doe in the headlights of a car.

"What ... what do you think you're ...?"

"Shut up," he said. "Save your talking for later ... when the pain starts."

He felt the knife in his hand bob as she swallowed dryly. The bus continued on, passing the Brenner house at thirty miles per hour. His parents wouldn't be home for two or three hours, maybe longer if they were working overtime. He could get a lot done by then, before they began missing him.

"Where are we going?" she finally asked.

"To your place," he told her.

They drove in silence for a full minute before she finally spoke again. "You know you're not going to get away with this, don't you?"

Cole laughed. He thought rather than said, *Oh, I will. You won't be able to identify me ... because you'll have no tongue to speak with or fingers to write with. Or eyes to pick me out of a lineup with.*

The yellow bus made its way off the paved roadway and onto a rutted dirt track with tall weeds and thistle growing to either side. For five more minutes, they traveled through dense woods of pine and oak that made up the southern half of Mangrum County. Then, eventually, they emerged into a clearing. They had arrived at Miss Anderson's place.

"Home Sweet Home," he whispered in her ear. He twisted the knife blade slightly, nicking the flesh just beneath her chin.

She flinched and her eyes grew even wider in the mirror.

Soon, the bus was parked. A moment later, the door was open and they were standing on solid ground. The place looked comfy and cozy, just what you might expect from a single woman on her own. A little white cottage with a green-shingled roof and a little yard out front, full rose bushes, flower beds, and statuary (gnomes, ceramic animals, birdhouses, and feeders). To the right of the house were a few outbuildings: a chicken coop, a woodshed, and a covered carport with a riding mower and a Nissan sedan parked beneath it.

"What now?" she asked. Her voice had a weird quality to it now. Soft and breathy. Was it terror? Or anticipation?

"Over there," he said, shoving her toward the shed.

Miss Anderson walked ahead of him, slowly, as if trying to think ... maybe attempting to figure out a way to escape. He grinned and jabbed her in the back with the tip of the knife, just below the right shoulder blade. Blood welled beneath her blouse, expanding as the material absorbed the crimson flow. She stumbled forward and muttered something beneath her breath.

What did she just say? he wondered, a little confused. *Did I hear her right? Did she just say ... "That feels good."?*

Onward they marched across the grass, toward the small building. To the right was a stacked rick of firewood, and to the left, a chopping stump. A hatchet was embedded in the top of the stump at an angle, old and red with rust.

"Come on!" he snapped at her. "You're wasting our time. I'm anxious to start this party. Aren't you?"

He watched her hang her head, as if in dejection and defeat. Cole grinned, then hauled off and kicked her in the small of the back. Miss Anderson grunted and stumbled forward. Her left hand went out, as if to break her fall or grab hold of something to regain her balance.

He saw, too late, that the thing she grabbed hold of was the hatchet.

Cole Brenner had absolutely no time to react. Miss Anderson was one fluid chain of motion. Grabbing the hickory handle, yanking the tool loose, swinging around ... and down.

Abruptly, the air in front of the boy was red. Spurting ... jetting ... a shower of crimson droplets. Stunned, he looked down and saw his right hand bucking and jerking in the grass, still holding the folding knife.

He felt Miss Anderson's tiny hand grab him by front of his t-shirt. Considering her size, she possessed more strength than he could have imagined. The woman slung him around, and soon *he* was stumbling, staggering toward the shed ... not her.

He glanced over his shoulder, heart pounding, wondering what had gone wrong in such a short period of time. Miss Anderson smiled cheerfully; her face flushed with excitement. Her eyes were what disturbed him the most. They were like stones. Flat, expressionless ... dead. She raised the hatchet to her mouth and ran her tongue along the damp metal, dislodging some of the crust that he now realized was not rust at all. He watched in horror as she swirled him around in her mouth and swallowed him hungrily.

"You've been a very naughty boy, Mr. Brenner," she said in a sweet voice laced with poison and sharp edges. "Time for a trip to the woodshed."

As Cole neared the weathered structure, his nostrils flared with the stench of blood and decay and his ears were filled with steely jingle of chains bearing the weight of things heavy and dead ... slowly swinging and turning in the darkness that awaited him within.

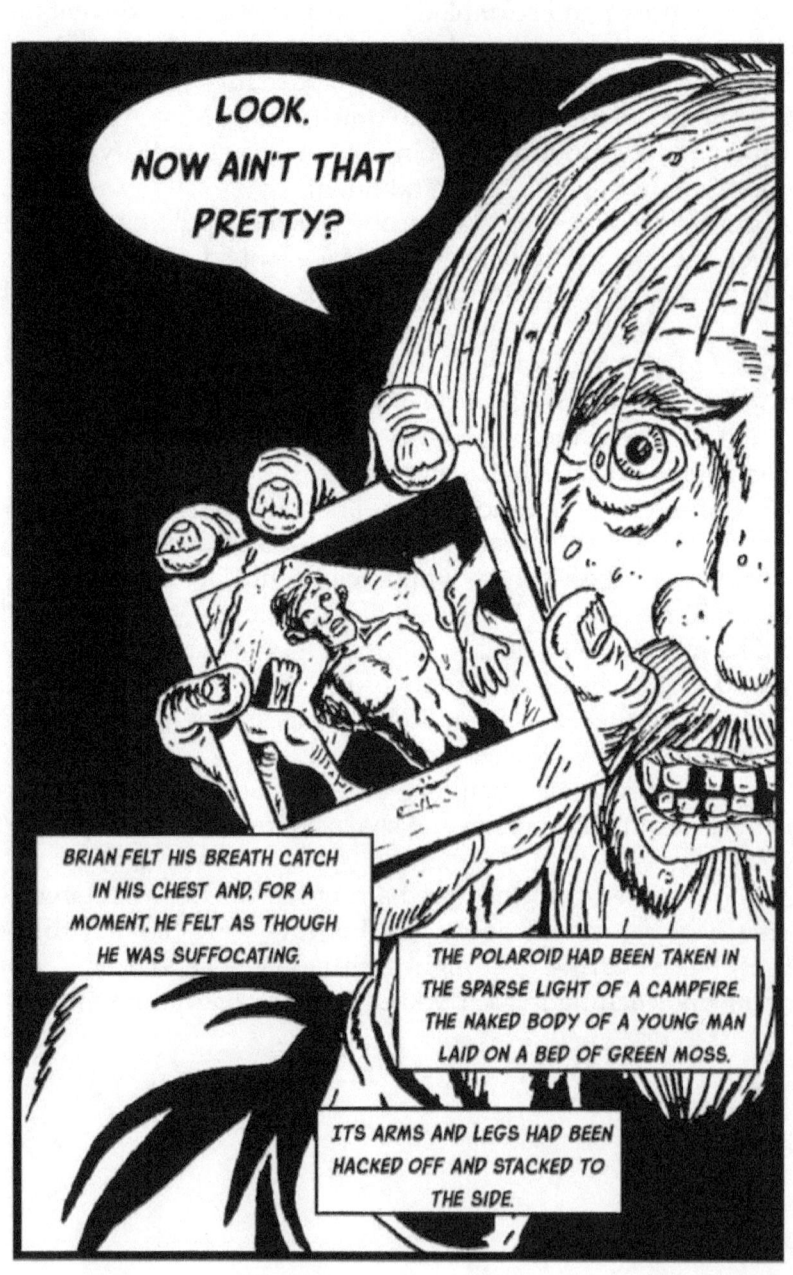

EXIT 85

Brian glanced at the gas gauge again. The needle was angled downward, dangerously close to the E mark.

He sighed and stared through the windshield. Interstate 75 stretched ahead, the flat black pavement illuminated by the van's headlights and nothing more. There was no moon to speak of that night. The swampy Florida terrain on either side of the interstate was cloaked in darkness. As far as he could tell, there wasn't a single streetlight in sight, or even the lighted window of a distant house. There was only the pale swath of the Windstar's headlights and the bright reflective markers that separated the two northbound lanes.

Brian tried to keep his annoyance to a minimum and glanced around at the other members of the Reid family. His wife, Jenny, was asleep in the passenger seat, her pretty face turned away from him. In the back, his two children also slept. Five-year-old Kendall was dozing beneath the restraints of his seatbelt, his Mickey Mouse ears cocked haphazardly over his eyes. The baby, Anne, who was barely over a year old, slept peacefully in her car seat, still wearing the Winnie the Pooh bib they had purchased at one of the Magic Kingdom souvenir shops.

He began to regret his decision to leave Florida that evening. Looking back, he knew they should have stayed the night in Orlando and gotten a fresh start the following morning. But after a week at Disney World, they had all pretty much been burnt out and were more than ready to get back home to Illinois.

The one thing Brian Reid hadn't bargained for was the long stretches of desolation between the interstate exits. It hadn't seemed so bad during the drive down, in broad daylight. But in the dead of night, the remote areas seemed to go on endlessly. He had driven for nearly fifteen miles since passing Exit 84, and now he wished he had stopped at the Amoco station there, like Jenny had suggested. Now his gas tank was almost dry and there wasn't a gas station in sight.

Brian reached for the radio and flipped the dial from one station to another, an annoying habit his wife had tried to break him of during their six years of marriage. A minute later he came upon a fuzzy classic rock station. Pink Floyd drifted softly through the van's speaker system as he continued down the road.

He was about to give up hope, when he spotted the reflective green rectangle of an exit sign up ahead. He was nearly upon the sign before he could read what was written on it.

EXIT 85
JASPER—DEFUNIAK SPRINGS
½ MILE

"Finally," he murmured beneath his breath. He spotted the exit ramp ahead and, switching on his turn signal, veered into the far right lane.

Thirty seconds later, he was off the interstate and crossing an overpass to a

gathering of unlit buildings with equally dark signs. He saw the round, star-emblazoned sign of an old Texaco station and headed toward it, keeping his fingers crossed on the steering wheel.

Brian pulled off the road and studied the station as he braked to a halt. There was a pale light in the station office, as well as lights shining through the small, greasy windows of the two auto repair bays. Was someone on duty, or was he just being overly optimistic?

"Aw, come on," he grumbled quietly. "I'm desperate here." He sighed again, then cut the van's engine to conserve what little fuel he had left. Jenny and the kids seemed oblivious to the stop. They continued to sleep soundly.

Brian climbed out of the van and stretched, feeling the bones of his lower spine crackle. He closed the door quietly and looked around. The Texaco station was the only building on the left side of the road. On the opposite side were two other businesses—a greasy spoon café and a convenience store... both closed. Further down the road was a large billboard lit by a couple of spotlights. It read:

BOB'S GATOR FARM—LIVE ALLIGATORS & REPTILES
SWAMP CURIOSITIES & SOUVENIRS
FLORIDA ORANGES & SALTWATER TAFFY—3 MILES AHEAD

He turned back to the gas station. Brian was still uncertain whether the business was open or closed. He walked to the office and tried the door. It was locked. "I guess that answers my question."

He was passing the gas pumps and starting back to the van when he heard a noise echoing from the far side of the station. He turned and caught a glimpse of someone rounding the corner, merging with the darkness beyond.

Maybe he wasn't wasting his time after all.

He walked toward the end of the building. The night was muggy and his sport shirt clung damply to his back and beneath his armpits. An unpleasant smell hung in the air, a gassy odor like rotting vegetation.

A moment later, he was peering around the corner. At the rear of the station, a single sixty-watt bulb glowed in the darkness. A cloud of candle flies and mosquitoes swarmed around the dull, yellow light.

"Hello?" he called out. "Is anyone back there?"

At first, he heard only the reedy chirring of crickets in the tall grass. Then a coarse voice answered him. "Come on back," it invited.

Brian stepped around several old car batteries and bent wheel rims as he made his way toward the rear of the building. When he got there, he found the station's back lot to be just as junky as the side was. Crushed heaps of wrecked cars stretched off into the inky darkness and, closer to the station, stood stacks of bald tires and large hunks of busted concrete with rusty lengths of steel reinforcement protruding from them. There were also plenty of aluminum soda cans and beer bottles lying around.

For a moment, he couldn't locate the one who had spoken. "Where are you?" he asked, a little louder than before.

Movement came again, this time from the shadows between two stacks of retreads. "Over here."

Brian suddenly felt as though he had made a mistake. He watched as the tall, lanky man stepped into the pale glow of the back door light. He was unshaven, with dirty blond hair and an even dirtier Atlanta Braves baseball cap. He was dressed in a ragged white undershirt, faded jeans, and a pair of Reeboks that looked on the verge of falling apart at the seams.

"Uh, do you work here?" Brian asked.

"Hell naw," said the man, eyeing the tourist carefully. "I was just camped out back here when I heard you pull up."

"Well, then, I'm sorry I woke you," apologized Brian.

He was about to leave, when the man reached into the back pocket of his jeans and took out a worn leather wallet. "Come here."

"What?"

"I said come here," the man said. "I got something to show you."

"I really have to go—"

A peculiar expression crossed the man's stubbled face. "I said for you to *come here* and *look*."

Brian's uneasiness suddenly changed into fear. He wanted to turn and run, but he wasn't sure that was a wise thing to do. The man continued to watch him, as though studying the expression on his face and gauging every little move he made.

"Are you coming?"

"Yeah," said Brian nervously. "Sure."

Cautiously, he walked over to the man. The strong stench of sweat and unwashed clothing was nearly overpowering. But he gave no indication that the man's lack of cleanliness was offensive to him. He sensed he would be making a bad mistake if he did.

The man grinned as he opened the flap and slowly rummaged through the contents of his wallet. Brian spotted a couple of worn dollar bills and some scraps of paper. And something else... a wrinkled Polaroid snapshot nestled in the middle of it all.

"You wanna see something you ain't never seen before?" he asked, his voice a husky whisper. He looked the tourist square in the eyes.

Brian was suddenly aware of the uneven quality of his gaze. The left eye was bloodshot and sickly looking, while the right was almost too normal in appearance. In fact, there wasn't a red vein or imperfection of any kind. It practically *shined* in the yellow light of the backdoor lamp and when the other eye moved, it remained fixed and steady. It was a second before Brian realized that the man's right orb was made of glass.

"Well, do you wanna see it or not?"

Brian simply swallowed dryly and nodded. He had the feeling that he had better agree... with whatever the man had to say.

The man chuckled softly and withdrew the photo. "Look. Now ain't that pretty?"

Brian felt his breath catch in his chest and, for a moment, he felt as though he was suffocating.

The Polaroid had been taken in the sparse light of a campfire. The naked body of a young man, perhaps sixteen or seventeen years of age, laid on a bed of green moss. Its arms and legs had been hacked off and stacked in a heap to the side.

"That's my doing, you know," rasped the man. Pride gleamed in his one good eye. "Took that picture no more'n a month ago. Not far from here, either."

A mosquito landed on the side of Brian's neck and bit him, but he made no move to shoo the bug away. *You're insane,* Brian wanted to say, but he didn't. He didn't dare.

The man with the filthy blond hair and glass eye scowled and stuck the photograph back in his wallet. "Now don't you git to acting like everyone else I've shown this to."

Brian felt as though he were caught up in a nightmare. He began to back away slowly.

Faster than he would have expected, the man leapt around him, blocking his way. He drew something from a pouch on his belt--a folding pocketknife. He opened it with a flip of his wrist. It was a movement he seemed to be very adept at. A six-inch blade of razor sharpness snapped into view, its steel flat gleaming in the yellowish light.

"Now, you just hold up for a second, hoss," he said with an ugly grin.

"What... what do you want?' Brian managed to say. His heart pounded wildly in his chest.

"Well, if I ain't mistaken, what I *want* is in that van out yonder."

Cold dread bloomed in the pit of Brian's stomach. "My wife?"

"No." The man's grin grew thinner and broader. "The baby."

Brian opened his mouth to reply but found that he couldn't.

"Looks about the right age to me," the man said. "About a year old, I'd guess."

"Yes," croaked Brian, although he couldn't figure out why he had answered.

The man licked his lips absently. "Ah, just tender enough. Over a slow fire with a little salt and pepper for seasoning. Maybe some wild onion on the side. You take it from me... there ain't nothing better."

Brian suddenly realized what the man was referring to. The very thought chilled him to the depths of his soul.

"Once I get rid of you, I reckon there won't be nothing stopping me," explained the lanky fellow. "The woman will be dead before she even wakes up. The other young'un might scream a bit... but, hey, let him holler. Nobody's around to hear him anyhow."

He's going to kill me, Brian thought, his mind reeling. *He'll kill Jenny and Kendall, too. And then he's... oh, God... he's going to take Anne and—*

The man took a slow step toward him. "Now let's hurry this up a bit, okay? It's getting late and I ain't had a bite all—"

Brian hurled himself at the man. He swung blindly at the man's face and felt his fist strike the bristled flat of his jaw. The man stumbled backward, then grinned and lashed out. The blade of the knife missed Brian the first time but skimmed across his forearm the second. A sharp sting sent Brian into immediate retreat.

"I was gonna make this easy for you, son," the man told him. "But I reckon I'll just have to make it a little more interesting, since you're so all-fired anxious to get in my way."

Again, a burst of terror and rage surged through Brian. With a yell, he launched himself at the man. He caught him by the wrist and slammed it against the gas station wall several times. Finally, his fingers splayed open and the knife went spinning into the darkness.

"You ain't quite what I expected, boy," laughed the man. "But then I reckon I ain't what you expected either." He reached up with his free hand and grabbed hold of Brian's throat. His grubby fingers burrowed into his skin, as though attempting to poke through.

Brian felt his windpipe begin to close and, for a second, couldn't catch his breath. He knew the man was on the verge of killing him. But then he thought of his wife and two children in the Windstar and he knew he had to do something… fast… before he lost consciousness. He kicked out frantically with his left foot and finally managed to trip his assailant.

The man lost his balance and went down. There was a hollow *thunk* as his head struck one of the concrete blocks. Blood trickled from his ears as he moaned and rolled over, struggling to his hands and knees. He reached out blindly with one hand and found a discarded Bud Lite bottle. He curled his fingers around the neck and broke it against the hard ground. Light gleamed wickedly along the jagged brown glass.

"No," Brian whispered. He dropped to his knees, took the man's head in both hands, and drove it face down against the concrete block… forcing it upon one of the steel reinforcement rods.

There was a moment of resistance at first. Then there was a moist *pop* and Brian felt something hit his chest. The man's head slid downward until it could go no further.

Slowly, Brian stood up. The man's arms and legs twitched violently for fifteen seconds, then abruptly grew still. A long sigh of air hissed through his clenched teeth, then only the monotonous tune of crickets filled the night air.

Brian simply stood where he was and watched, half expecting the man to get up. But he didn't. And he never would.

The horror of what had just taken place finally sank in. Brian quickly left that awful place, stumbling through the junk along the side of the gas station and heading for the van.

He prayed that his family would still be asleep when he got there. And they were. All three dozed peacefully, unaware of how very close to death they had come.

Brian climbed into the van and gently closed the door. Then he started the engine and pulled away from the Texaco station.

As he was heading down the exit ramp, back to I-75, Brian knew for the first time in his life how a hit-and-run driver might feel.

Soon, the van was again heading northward for the Florida state line. He cut off the air conditioner and rolled down his window, letting the wind dry the sweat from his face. It wasn't long before his pulse and breathing had returned to normal.

A minute or so passed before he realized that something was pressing uncomfortably against his chest. He dipped his fingers into the breast pocket of his sport shirt and found something there that shouldn't have been. Something hard and round.

He held it to the pale green glow of the dashboard light. The object between his fingers stared at him, almost accusingly so.

Quickly, he flung the glass eye out the van window. It hit the rushing surface of the blacktop with a brittle crack, then was gone.

Brian felt along the Windstar's console blindly, until he found the packet of pre-moistened wipes that Jenny kept handy for little Anne. He shucked one from the sleeve and wiped his hands, fighting down nausea as he did.

Then he felt a small sting and remembered the cut on his forearm. Almost afraid to look, he turned his arm in the muted light. He expected to find a large gash, but, instead, there was only a thin line of blood, no more than two inches in length. He dabbed at the cut with the towelette, then tossed the damp cloth out the window.

It was so horribly absurd that he nearly laughed out loud. A brutal fight to the death and all he had come away with was an injury the equivalent of a paper cut.

Onward he drove into the Florida darkness, keeping one eye on the gas gauge and praying he would make it to the next exit.

Brian knew his wife would ask about the cut on his arm sooner or later.

He had until sunrise to come up with the right answer.

BURNING BRIDGES

"There it is," said Charlie Powell. "Up ahead." The deputy gunned the engine and sent the Trenton County patrol car down the desolate stretch of Brookhollow Road.

Sheriff Buck Ballard leaned forward in the passenger seat and peered through the windshield. A ball of fire lit up the night a quarter mile away. It blazed like a funeral pyre against the darkness of the rural countryside. If it was what they suspected, that was exactly what it was.

Soon, they were coming up on the scene fast and both lawmen could tell it was a car consumed by flames.

"Dammit!" said Buck. "Not another one!"

They pulled onto the gravel shoulder of the narrow road and emerged from the cruiser, squinting against the glare and heat. The volunteer fire department had beaten them there. Or, rather, the fire chief had. Sonny Bumpus had the big engine pulled to the side just beyond the burning vehicle. The emergency vehicle was practically an antique in make and model, but as solid and dependable as an iron horse.

"How long have you been here, Sonny?" Buck called to him, keeping a safe distance from the fire.

"Just a minute or so," said the chief. "I set off the alarm when I heard the explosion from the fire hall. Must've been the tank blowing." Sonny's homely face was tomato red and full of frustration. "The nearest hookup is a good mile away. We're going to have to try smothering with KCl." He took a couple of large extinguishers from the back of the truck and handed one to the sheriff. "Damn those guys. They should've been here by now. Can't find volunteers worth a shit these days!"

"Calm down, Sonny," Buck said grimly. "This isn't a life-and-death situation. Not anymore."

It took some doing, and a couple more canisters of potassium chloride, but they finally got the blaze under control and extinguished. The brilliance of the fire was suddenly gone and the darkness of the Tennessee night crowded in, leaving only a full moon overhead and the flashing lights of the two emergency vehicles to shed further light on the scene of the accident.

No, thought the sheriff. *Scene of the crime.* He had to keep convincing himself of that fact, given the evidence of the last incident.

Buck and Sonny tossed their spent extinguishers away and stood there examining the wreckage. The vehicle appeared to be a Ford SUV, maybe a Bronco or Explorer. The hull was black and smoldering and the frame was twisted like a horseshoe. It looked as though it had been broadsided by a freight train.

"Beat all the hell… just like the other one." Buck turned to his deputy. "Charlie… any idea who it belongs to?"

Deputy Powell circled the steaming hull. "The plate is scorched, but I can make out the numbers. I'll put in a call to the DMV and find out who it's registered to."

As Charlie headed back to the car, Buck took a flashlight from his belt and directed the beam of the flashlight inside. Amid the smoky vapor, he saw two blackened bodies sitting upright in the front. They seem to be misshapen. The sheriff examined the back seat, praying that it would be empty.

It wasn't. There was a small, charred form curled upon the burnt upholstery and springs.

"Oh God. There's a *kid* in there."

He looked over to see if Sonny Bumpus had heard him. He had. The chief stood there, face as pale as a bedsheet. He shook his head silently, his eyes shiny and close to tears. "Dear Lord, Buck… why? Who would do such a thing?"

Buck turned away from wreckage and regarded the man. Sonny was a good man, a man who had beaten the odds of a white trash upbringing and poor education and gained the respect of the folks of Trenton County. Buck remembered Sonny from his childhood days. He had been a shy, awkward boy who spent most of his time barefoot and clad in hand-me-down overalls. Everywhere he had gone in the little town of Iver's Junction, his scrawny redbone hound tagged along. Buck picked his brains for the name of the hound. Old Britches, that's what Sonny had called him. The dog had been given that name because his hindquarters were so eaten up with mange that it looked like he was wearing a pair of bright pink pants.

Buck simply shook his head, having no answer to give.

"Boss."

The sheriff turned to see Charlie's stricken face. He looked like he was about to puke. "It's registered to Joe Cochran."

Buck thought of the three mangled and charred masses in the hull of the vehicle. "Lord have mercy! Joe and Betty... and their little boy."

Charlie was shocked. "Tommy? You mean Tommy was in there, too. Isn't he a friend of your boy?"

Buck nodded. "His best friend. Has been since kindergarten."

The deputy stared at the smoldering SUV. "What the hell's going on here, Buck? Who's doing this?"

Silently, the lawman stared off into the night. He didn't answer Charlie. He couldn't. He himself had no earthly idea who was responsible. Or, even worse, what unearthly reason they might have for doing such a thing.

Emily was still up when Buck dragged home around two-thirty that morning. She sat at the kitchen table with a mug of coffee and an Amish romance novel.

His wife left her chair and embraced him. His clothing was heavy with the odor of smoke and extinguisher chemical. He stiffened at first, then sighed and rested his chin on her shoulder.

"Was it bad? I heard some of it on the scanner, but..."

"It was," he told her. "Emily... it was the Cochrans."

The woman pulled away and stared at him. "Oh, God, *no!* Joe and Betty..."

Buck's heart felt like a stone in his chest. "And..."

Tears came easily for Emily. They came quickly now. "Oh, Buck... oh no... not..."

He nodded. "Tommy."

She sat heavily in her kitchen chair. The news hit her hard. She was practically a second mother to the boy. "How are we going to tell David?"

"I don't know," admitted Buck. "They were like twins... practically joined at the hip."

Emily shook her head in disbelief. "You don't believe this is an accident, do you? Like the other one? You think that some crazy son of a bitch is..."

As if in answer, Buck's cell phone rang.

Buck and Emily looked at one another. "You don't think—?"

The sheriff nodded, letting the phone in his pocket ring a second time, then a third. "Yes... I'm afraid it is."

He hesitated, thinking of the call he had received directly after they had discovered Rollie and Mary Lou Baker, mangled and roasted, in their Nissan Altima two nights before. Then he answered it. "Hello?"

There was silence at first, then the sound of weeping. The sound of a man crying softly on the other end of the line.

"Bridges," moaned his trembling voice. *"Burning bridges!"*

"Who is this?" the sheriff demanded. Then he cursed as the call was terminated and only silence pressed against his ear.

"Was it *him*?"

"Yes. And he said the same thing as before."

"Burning bridges," his wife said. "But what does it mean? That usually means finishing something and then moving on... not doing the horrible thing over and over again."

The following day, the state forensic lab sent Buck its findings on the two burnt and wrecked vehicles, as well as autopsy reports for both the Baker and Cochran families.

The sheriff sat there in his office on the ground floor of the county courthouse and read the coroner's report several times, shaking his head in disbelief. "This can't be right," he told himself, then decided to put in a call to the Nashville pathologist and clarify a few things.

He felt a little hesitant questioning the judgment of Dr. Walter Harris, given the excellent work had done for the state justice department for the past thirty years, but there were several facts presented in the reports that seemed too strange to accept from a mere typewritten summation.

A few minutes later, he had the coroner on the phone. "Excuse me, Dr. Harris, but this is Sheriff Ballard in Iver's Junction. I have some questions concerning the autopsies you performed on the Baker and Cochran families."

"I'll certainly be glad to verify any of my conclusions for you, Sheriff," said the pathologist. "What do you want to know?"

"Well, the Baker autopsies for instance. It says here that the previous suspicion of the bodies having been dismembered and mutilated by the force of the car crash was proven to be false. That something other than vehicular impact caused the fatalities."

"Yes. As the report shows, the wounds were not caused by jagged metal or glass. Rather, from the breadth and depth of the incisions, I determined that they were made by a heavy, edged implement, most likely a broad axe. Also, the wounds were inflicted during a period of time between the actual crash and the fire afterward. My conclusion is that someone hacked the Bakers to death shortly after their automobile had been incapacitated."

"And these findings apply to the Cochran family as well?"

"Yes. Both Joe and Betty Cochran were brutally hacked to death. The child, on the other hand, suffered only a single blow to the skull. It was clearly intended to be a killing blow, but not as savage as those the parents were subjected to."

Buck flipped a page and found another puzzling point of interest. "One other thing, Doctor. This must have been a mistake, but it says here that traces of kerosene were found on the remains of the victims. You mean gasoline, don't you? From the rupturing of the gas tanks?"

"No, I'm afraid that point is quite conclusive," said Walter Harris. "Whoever it was that killed these people—and there is no doubt that their deaths were premeditated and not merely accidental—the murderer soaked his victims with kerosene prior to setting them and their vehicles ablaze."

That afternoon, Buck drove out to the crash site on Brookhollow Road.

All that was left of the incident two nights ago was a broad, black patch of scorched pavement to show where the SUV had rested. He left his patrol car and stood there on the empty stretch of road for a while, studying the stretch of rural blacktop, which stretched from Highway 70, clear to the Trenton County line, five miles away. To one side of Brookhollow stood a tall stand of dense thicket and woods, while to the other yawned broad pastureland beyond a barrier of barbed wire fencing. A small herd of black angus grazed in the shade of a spreading chestnut tree a hundred yards away.

The sheriff crouched and studied the pavement. There were heavy skid marks on the asphalt, leading a good fifty feet from the spot where the Cochran vehicle had burned. It almost looked like the SUV had lost control at some point and that the impact had taken place somewhere else. He walked along the roadway until he found bits of glass, as well as a few fragments of twisted metal.

Buck looked toward the far side of the road. A dirt turnoff was located directly across from the point of impact. An old logging road that disappeared into the woods.

The sheriff walked over and studied the earth of the road. The ground was dry, the dirt powdery. A few tire tracks, but they were fragmented, useless. In the weeds to the left of the road he discovered half a dozen cigarette butts. Someone had waited a long time before the Cochrans had shown up. They had sat there and smoked for at least an hour or two.

As he returned to his car, he spotted something lying in a drainage ditch that ran along the pasture side of the road. He jumped down into the ditch and retrieved the bundle. It was a large canvas tarpaulin--camouflage print, about ten-by-fifteen feet. A common enough item in Tennessee, every other hunter in the county owned one. But this one was different. As he examined it, he found traces of white paint and fragments of safety glass on one side. The Cochrans' Ford had sported a white paint job before the fire had burned it away.

On the other side were traces of red paint, as well as a few chrome flakes that had been shaved off a bumper.

Buck carefully folded the tarp and carried it to his patrol car, then stashed it in the trunk. Buck was merely a rural sheriff with no experience in the type of crime he was now facing. Still, he had his suspicions about what had taken place on Brookhollow Road.

More than anything else, it was the lack of motive that bugged the hell out of him. No matter how hard he tried, he simply couldn't come up with one.

That evening, Buck was driving home from the office, when he passed Eddie's Tavern, a local honky-tonk that was located three miles southwest of town on Highway 70. He was anxious to get home and drive the bizarre case of the Bakers and Cochrans out of his mind, at least until tomorrow morning. But something caused him to slow his patrol car, make a U-turn, and go back.

Rudy Shelton's big dump truck was parked in the gravel lot. Buck pulled up next to the vehicle and got out. He circled the dump truck, studying it with interest. It was a big Mack with a red cab and dusty metal bed. Rudy worked for Taylor's Quarry across the county line and drove the truck home, for lack of a vehicle of his own.

The cab of the truck was covered with dents and scratches. Much of its red paint was gone from the front fenders and the foremost edge of the hood. Also, the dome of one of the headlights was cracked.

Of course, that could turn out to mean absolutely nothing. Most of Taylor's fleet of trucks was in similar shape, some even worse than this one. It was the driver himself that raised a red flag of suspicion in Buck Ballard's mind.

Rudy Shelton was known throughout Trenton County as a drunkard and a troublemaker. Buck had arrested Rudy for everything from DUI to wife beating. But the most serious charge had been arson. Five years ago, Rudy had made an agreement with a drinking buddy to help set his house on fire for the insurance money. Rudy had been paid three hundred dollars in cash and a deer rifle to do the job but had been convicted of the crime for one simple and stupid slipup. Rudy's wallet had fallen from his hip pocket after the blaze had been set and it was found lying in the driveway the following morning. The crime had netted Rudy a sentence of two to six years in the state pen, but he had only served eighteen months due to a record of good behavior and a compassionate parole board.

Buck examined the truck a few moments more, then walked into the tavern. He found Rudy sitting at the bar, smoking and nursing a longneck Miller. Eddie Burton, the proprietor, stood behind the bar, dusting a red and blue neon Budweiser sign with a bar rag.

The sheriff climbed onto the stool next to the quarry worker. "Hey, Rudy."

The big man with the rusty red beard and the Tennessee Vols baseball cap looked over and grunted. A look of disgust crossed his face as he raised the beer bottle and took another swallow.

"What can I get you, Buck?" asked Eddie.

"I'm off duty, but I'm on my way home," said Buck. "Emily would brain me with a frying pan if I showed up with beer on my breath. Besides, I just dropped in to talk to Rudy here."

Shelton turned his head and glared at the lawman. "Talk to me about *what*, Ballard?"

"Oh, I was just wondering how you've been lately," he replied. "Been keeping out of trouble?"

"Hell, yeah, I've been keeping out of trouble!" grumbled Rudy. "Not that it's any of your damned business!"

Buck watched as Rudy ground the butt of his cigarette into a glass ashtray, then fetched a pack of Marlboro 100's from the pocket of his gray work shirt. The sheriff recalled another point of interest in the forensic lab's report. The cigarette butts Buck had discovered near the scene of the Cochran crash had also been Marlboros.

"Wonder if I could ask you a question, Rudy?"

Shelton shrugged. "It's a free country."

"Where were you this past Monday night?"

Rudy stared at him. "I was home with the old lady, watching TV."

"How about Saturday night?"

Anger began to flare in the man's eyes. "I was right here, from seven till closing. Did some drinking and played pool with my buddies."

"Yep," said the bartender. "Rudy was here till I locked up at two AM."

Rudy's eyes narrowed. "What the hell are you getting at, Ballard?"

"Nothing," said Buck, leaving his stool. "Just curious, that's all."

The man's face turned a deep shade of red. "You think maybe I had something to do with what happened out on Brookhollow Road, don't you?"

The sheriff simply walked toward the door. "See you around, Rudy," he called back to the man at the bar. Then he left the tavern.

Buck took another long look at the dump truck, then climbed into his patrol car and pulled out onto the highway. He felt a little foolish about going into Eddie's and grilling Rudy like that. Shelton wasn't one of Buck's favorite people and vice versa. But he didn't think Rudy would be involved in something as serious and sinister as this. And, besides, despite the man's shortcomings, he would never kill a child. He simply didn't have it in him.

Come to think of it, no one in Trenton County was cold-hearted enough to commit such a horrible crime.

Or, at least, no one appeared to be.

Sheriff Ballard and Deputy Powell sat in a rear booth of Betsie's Café on Thursday night, drinking coffee and winding down after a hectic day.

The worse part had been the multiple funerals that had taken place at the cemetery next to the Iver's Junction Baptist Church. First, the Bakers that morning and then the Cochrans later that afternoon. Buring one person in such a small community was bad enough, but burying five in one day was devastating, especially when one of the dearly departed was an innocent, seven-year-old child.

Buck recalled the latter service all too vividly; the tears, the hollow-eyed states, all possessed a common anguish just beneath the sorrow. His son, David, who had been Tommy Cochran's best friend, was taking it hard and it hurt Buck to no end to see the extent of the boy's grief. Standing next to the last grave as the undersized casket

was lowered into Tennessee clay, Buck vowed that he would work
night and day if necessary to find the one responsible. He hadn't heard
Charlie say so, but he could tell by the haunted look in his deputy's
eyes that he felt the same way.

They had gone over the details of the two incidents that evening
and had come to the same conclusion. Both families, the Bakers as well
as the Cochrans, had been traveling along Brookhollow Road when
they were confronted by a vehicle of great size and weight—perhaps
a tractor-trailer or dump truck—somewhere along the twelve mile
stretch of rural road. Their vehicles were smashed into immobility
and the occupants brutally murdered while they were still dazed by
the unexpected crash. Both families had been killed by multiple blows
from an axe. After the deaths of the victims, the assailant had doused
their bodies with kerosene, setting both them and their vehicles on
fire. Then the sick son of a bitch had gone his merry way.

Following his suspicion of Rudy Shelton, Buck had wracked his
brain trying to figure out exactly who in Trenton County might be
capable of performing such heinous acts. He could think of absolutely
no one. Iver's Junction was a quaint, God-fearing Southern town, full
of friendly neighbors who were forever anxious to lend a helping
hand.

But obviously someone in the close-knit community was not who
they appeared to be. Buck couldn't shake the feeling that there was
a depraved monster living among them, perhaps someone he passed
on the street every day of the week. Perhaps even someone he called
a friend.

Buck and Charlie were paying their tabs at the front counter when
a high-pitched wail split the night air outside. "Isn't that the siren
over at the fire hall?" asked Betsie from behind the cash register.

The two lawmen looked at one another. They told Betsie to keep
the change and headed for their patrol car. They were climbing into
the cruiser when the radio crackled into life and the voice of Sonny
Bumpus came from the speaker. "Sheriff? Are you there?"

Buck picked up the mike. "Yeah, I'm here, Chief. What's up?"

For a moment, only static echoed across the airwaves, then Sonny
answered. "I'm afraid it's happened again. We got another one on
Brookhollow, about a quarter mile past the Indian Creek Bridge."

It was past one in the morning when Buck and Charlie finally returned to town. They entered the office, pale-faced and emotionally drained. Buck slumped wearily into the chair behind his desk, while Charlie fired up the coffee maker. Neither man spoke, for there was really nothing more to be said that night. The sobering memory of gruesome death preyed on their minds like a buzzard picking at fresh roadkill. And no matter how hard they tried, they simply couldn't drive the images of the past few hours from their thoughts.

This one had been the worst of the bunch. Bubba McGill and his girlfriend, Tracie Bush, their Chevy pickup forced off the road, their bodies brutally hacked open, then burned beyond recognition.

Buck closed his eyes and sighed. The state police had left the scene an hour before, as well as the volunteer firefighters. He and Charlie had lingered and watched as the county paramedics transferred the smoldering remains into glossy black bags and carried them to the ambulance that would take them to Nashville and the inquisitive scalpel of Dr. Harris the following morning.

The sheriff was jarred from his thoughts by the telephone. Charlie crossed the outer office and answered it on the third ring. "Buck, it's your wife."

Buck nodded and picked up the phone on his desk. "Hi, honey. What are you doing up?"

There was a moment of silence, then Emily spoke. "Buck, I just got a call a moment ago."

The sheriff straightened up in his chair. "Was it *him*?"

"Yes, I believe so."

"Okay, thanks for letting me know. I'll be home in a little while."

They said their goodbyes, then Buck hung up and sat there, staring expectantly at the telephone. Charlie brought a mug of black coffee and set it on the desk in front of him. Then he fetched a chair next to a file cabinet and joined Buck as he waited.

A minute hadn't passed when the phone rang again.

Buck exchanged a knowing glance with Charlie, then answered it. "Hello?"

A ragged, mournful sob, then—
"Burning bridges..."

The next day, Buck drove down Brookhollow Road, running an idea over in his mind. He had awoken early that morning with a suspicion nagging at him and, by the time he had finished breakfast, he knew he had to check it out. If not, he'd never get any work done that day.

From the beginning, he had failed to see one connecting factor in all the killings and he felt foolish for not realizing it in the first place. The Bakers, the Cochrans, McGill and his girlfriend—all lived along the rural stretch of Brookhollow Road.

Exactly why that factored into their grisly murders was another question that bugged him. Certainly the fact that all of their residences were located on Brookhollow gave the murderer ample opportunity to strike while they were on their way to and from town. But what was the motive? What reason did the killer have for wanting to destroy those people and their vehicles so viciously?

Buck could only think of two possibilities. One had to do with several of the victims themselves. Rollie Baker, Joe Cochran, and Bubba McGill had all grown up together, attended the same high school, and been on the Trenton County High football team. What that connection might have to do with the murders, he had no earthly idea. It just seemed like too strange of coincidence to dismiss.

And then there was another factor to consider, one that made a little more sense. The Bakers' and the Cochrans' farms were divided by the property of a man named Harry Jones. Jones had tried several times in the past to buy both farms on Brookhollow Road, but neither man would agree to sell. The refusals had angered Jones and created some bad blood between him and his neighbors. It certainly wasn't a private grudge. Whenever Harry got liquored up at Eddie's place, he enjoyed badmouthing Rollie and Joe for their unwillingness to sell out.

Could that be what was going on? Had Jones finally found the nerve to get even with the two farmers, thinking that their deaths would assure him a fair bid at their properties? Buck wasn't sure. There was still Bubba McGill to consider. Bubba had owned only a single acre of scrubby land at the far end of Brookhollow Road, and all that stood there was a single-wide trailer with junky cars parked around it. Bubba certainly owned nothing that Harry would be envious of. Nothing that he would be willing to commit murder for.

Buck reached the Jones farm and turned into the rutted dirt drive. Parked next to the barn was another reason why Harry might be a likely suspect. It was Harry's two-ton Ford flatbed truck, the one he used to haul ricks of firewood to his Trenton County customers. The truck was big and powerful… and had a bright red cab.

The sheriff left his patrol car and approached the truck from the rear. He checked the bed, which had wooden siderails and a back gate. A dozen ricks of dried maple were stacked along one side, covered by a canvas tarp. That wasn't what drew Buck's attention the most, however. Lying on the scarred floor of the truck bed was a greasy chainsaw, as well as an axe. A well-worn broad axe with a rusty head and a long handle of hard hickory.

Buck walked around to the front of the truck. The nose of the cab had been damaged recently. The grillwork was buckled in and one of the headlights was completely shattered.

"Sheriff," came a voice from a tool shed a few yards away.

Startled, Buck turned toward the building. Harry Jones stood near the doorway, dressed in grungy overalls and a flannel shirt. He sported a wiry black beard and a perpetual scowl on his homely face.

"How's it going, Harry?" he replied.

Jones eyed him suspiciously. "Something I can do for you?"

Buck shrugged. "Just thought I'd stop by for a minute. Haven't seen you in town for the past week or so."

"I've been busy," said Harry nodding toward the pile of wood in his truck. "Heard you've been busy, too. With that ugly business down the road a piece."

The lawman nodded. "Yeah, I have."

Harry frowned darkly. "Damn shame is what it is. I reckon folks know my opinion of Baker and Cochran, but that was just business. Never had no real hatred toward them. It just peeved me that they wouldn't sell out to me." He spat tobacco juice into the weeds next to the shed. "Awful what happened to them and their families. Just plain awful. Especially where poor Tommy Cochran was concerned."

Buck simply nodded again. Then he glanced at the front of the big flatbed. "By the way, what happened to your truck there, Harry?"

Jones stared at him for a long moment, with nary a shred of emotion on his face. "Hit a deer. A big white-tailed buck. Must've been a twelve-pointer, at least. Jumped right out of the trees and crossed in front of me. Didn't kill it, though. It stumbled, then limped off into the woods along Indian Creek. Didn't have my rifle with me, so I didn't have a chance to put it out of its misery. It tore the hell outta the front of my old truck, didn't it?"

"Did you report it to the game warden?"

Harry grinned with tobacco-stained teeth. "Sure did. He came out here and wrote up a report and everything. Even wrote down the damage done to my truck."

Buck noticed a cigarette pack peeking from the pocket of Jones's shirt. "Tell me something. What brand of cigarettes do you smoke?"

The man's eyes narrowed a bit. "If you're aiming to accuse me of something, Ballard, you'd best stop beating around the bush and do it."

Buck stared at the farmer for a long moment, then shook his head. "Don't have any cause to accuse you of anything, Harry… not right now, at least."

"Then why don't you just get the hell of my land," the man said flatly.

Buck nodded. "See you around, Harry. And be sure to fix that busted headlight. I'd hate to have to write you a ticket."

The sheriff climbed into his patrol car, backed out of the driveway, and then started back down Brookhollow Road for town. Buck knew he should have left the Jones farm with a better handle on his suspicions, but strangely enough he didn't. Most of it had to do with the expression in Harry Jones's eyes. He hadn't seen a trace of fear there, only angry indignation at the questions Buck had asked him.

He had gone to the Jones farm with a suspect in mind, but he was less sure now than he had been before.

On his way back to the office, Buck stopped by Weller's Hardware on

Main Street. Hugh Weller's store handled hardware and tools, as well as camping and fishing supplies, and a large selection of automotive parts. Buck had some questions to ask and, if anyone in Iver's Junction could answer them, it would be Hugh.

"So, what can I help you with, Buck?" asked the storekeeper, sucking on the end of his pipe. A bluish cloud of Borkum Riff hovered above Hugh's balding head.

"I need to know if someone's been in recently to buy a few particular items."

"Okay. What would that be?"

"First, has anyone bought kerosene?" Buck asked.

"Are you kidding? Half the county has kerosene space heaters in their barns and workshops. I reckon I've sold a couple hundred gallons so far this fall. What else?"

"How about a camouflage tarp? Canvas, about ten by twelve feet?"

"It's hunting season, Buck. I've sold dozens of them. Had to reorder, too." Hugh frowned. "I'm not helping any, am I?"

"What about headlamps for a big truck?" continued the sheriff, feeling as though he was grasping at straws.

"Yep, did sell a pair of those just the other day." Then he told him who had made the purchase.

Buck thought nothing of it. "How about red touch-up paint?"

Weller nodded. The buyer turned out to be the same one who had purchased the headlights.

"Well, thanks anyway, Hugh," said Buck as he turned to leave.

"Sorry I couldn't be more help," said the storeowner.

Buck left the shop and walked across Main Street to the courthouse, leaving his car parked where it was. He was almost to the courthouse steps when an elderly man named George Lovell left the building. George was a retired tobacco farmer who now spent most of his time making his rounds in Iver's Junction, drinking coffee in the café and chewing the fat with anyone who had the time and patience. George was decked out in crisp Duck Head overalls, a starched white shirt, and a gray felt hat. He walked with the help of a cane, but otherwise appeared as spry as a man half of his eighty-three years. Old Man Lovell was as much a constant in Trenton County as the changing of the seasons or the steady ticking of the courthouse clock.

"Well, Buck, have you found the one who's been stalking Brookhollow Road?" the elderly man asked as he reached the bottom of the steps.

"No sir," admitted the sheriff. "Haven't turned up hide nor hair of our vehicular Jack the Ripper."

George Lovell's friendly smile faded and his face suddenly grew serious. "Have you got a moment to sit down and talk a spell? I know you've got your hands full, but this could be important."

Buck shrugged. "Sure, why not?"

When they had found a place on a park bench beneath one of the courtyard's ancient oaks, George sat there gripping the crooked end of his walking cane. "You know, Buck, I've been around these parts for a long while, and in that time I've seen about everything that's happened in this town, both good and bad. Folks have been done wrong by one person or another along the way, but most of the really bad things that have been done in Iver's Junction have lost their bite and been forgotten... for the time being. I've been mulling those murders over in my mind and I figure that's what happened in this case. I figure that someone had a heap of hurting put on him years ago and he just recently gathered up the nerve to do something about it."

The sheriff studied the old man curiously. "Just what are you driving at, George?"

"What I'm saying, Buck, is that I think I know who your killer is. I wasn't sure at first... that's why I haven't spoken up until now. But the more I think on it, the more practical it seems." He noted the look of sudden interest in the lawman's eyes. "Matter of fact, I'm a little surprised you haven't figured it out for yourself. But, like I said before, folks tend to forget the really nasty things that go on during the course of a town's history. And, besides, you were only a kid at the time. But I want to tell you a story and, afterwards, I believe you'll get the picture, too."

"I'm all ears," said Buck.

George Lovell nodded, then started talking in that engrossing way he had with a tall-tale or local ghost story. Except that it wasn't a yarn that the old man was spinning this time. No, this was a true incident that had taken place nearly thirty years ago. And, halfway through the telling, Buck Ballard felt the shock of realization hit him. And, suddenly, he knew the identity of the Brookhollow murderer without a shadow of a doubt.

Kenny Shepard pulled his four-wheel-drive off the main highway and headed down the dark country road. There was no moon to speak of that night, and if there had been, it would have been hidden by a blanket of heavy storm clouds that hung overhead. Kenny didn't give a damn whether it rained or not. It was the butt-end of a Saturday night and, after an evening of drinking at Eddie's Tavern, all he intended to do was climb into bed and sleep through the church bells the following morning. He took a bottle of Wild Turkey from the floorboard, took a long swig of the liquor, and fiddled with the knob of the SUV's radio, searching for a country station.

He was a couple of miles down Brookhollow Road when he got the uneasy feeling that he was being followed. He glanced into the rearview mirror but found only pitch darkness dogging his bumper. Kenny took another swallow of whiskey, but still couldn't shake the feeling. He turned off the radio and listened. He could hear it now. The thunderous roar of a big engine less than fifty feet behind him.

Kenny slowed down a bit, letting the red glow of his brake light throw some light on the situation. "Good God Almighty!" he said and floored the gas pedal a second before a wall of canvas-covered steel could slam into the back of his Chevy Blazer. He suddenly thought of the horrible deaths that had plagued Brookhollow Road during the past two weeks and wondered if he was going to be the next one found mangled and burned to a cinder.

He heard his pursuer push his engine to the max and, suddenly, the dark mass of canvas again loomed in Kenny's rearview mirror. He couldn't avoid the collision this time. There was a teeth-rattling concussion as the vehicle slammed into the rear of the four-wheel-drive. Kenny heard the crumple and squeal of steel against steel, as well as the clatter of his bumper falling away and tumbling across the blacktop.

Frantically, Kenny sped up, but the other matched his speed. There was another tremendous crash and the back window imploded, peppering the nape of Kenny's neck with glass. He nearly lost control then, the Blazer veering dangerously close to a drainage ditch at the side of the road. He wrestled with the steering wheel and floored the accelerator until the sole of his foot ached with the effort.

Then, unexpectedly, another vehicle joined the chase. From out of a side road shot a single car. As it pulled along the dark juggernaut, flashing blue lights spiraled in the night and Kenny realized with relief that it was a Trenton County patrol car.

"Pull over!" the voice of Buck Ballard demanded through the cruiser's external speaker. "Pull over immediately! You are under arrest!"

The driver of the shadowy vehicle ignored the warning and jerked his wheel sharply to the right, slamming into the side of the police car hard enough to shear away a sideview mirror and knock one of the blue lights on the roof out of commission. In response, a shot was fired—the throaty blast of a shotgun from the sound of it—and the big vehicle's right front tire shredded beneath a hail of buckshot. Blue-white sparks sprayed into the night air as the wheel rim clashed with dusty asphalt. A moment later, the deadly vehicle slowed, then pulled to a halt at the side of the rural road.

Kenny Shepard eased his Blazer to the opposite side of Brookhollow Road and climbed out. The patrol car was parked a few yards to the rear. "Stay put, Kenny!' Buck called out to him. "Let us handle this!"

"The hell I will!" growled the man. He pulled a jack handle from beneath his seat and took an angry step into the roadway, intending to put a hurting on the lunatic that had tried to kill him that night.

Buck left the patrol car, then shucked his service revolver from its holster and started toward the front of the vehicle. At the same time, Sonny Bumpus bolted from the cab of the Trenton County volunteer fire engine, clad in a long black slicker and fire helmet. His eyes gleamed madly in the blue glow of the police lights and he searched the darkness until he spotted Kenny standing near his battered Blazer. With a wail of intense rage, Sonny lifted a long-handled broad axe in both hands and sprinted down the road toward his intended victim.

"Don't, Sonny!" warned Buck, aiming his revolver. "Stop right where you are!"

The fire chief ignored him. "Britches!" he screamed like a soul in torment. "They burned Old Britches!" He swung the deadly length of the axe back and forth, like an insane knight brandishing a broadsword.

"Dammit, Sonny... *stop!*" But no matter how loudly Buck pleaded, his warning fell on deaf ears. He lowered the muzzle of his revolver toward Sonny's legs and squeezed off a couple of shots. One of the .38 slugs caught the man just behind his left knee. Sonny stumbled, then fell to the roadway.

"Lay there and don't move a muscle!" yelled the sheriff.

But still Sonny wouldn't listen. He struggled to his knees and reached out for the axe, which had fallen from his grasp. He found the handle and began to struggle to his feet.

"Please, Sonny! *Stay down!*" Buck sensed Deputy Powell standing behind him, holding the shotgun that had disabled the murderous fire engine.

The fire chief looked toward Buck. There were tears in his wild eyes. "Old Britches!" he sobbed. *"They burnt Britches!"* Then he was back on his feet again and stumbling toward his intended victim.

Another shot ripped through the night. A dark circle appeared behind Sonny's left ear and he pitched forward for the last time. He hit the pavement hard, the axe dropping from his fingers, and laid there without moving.

With a sinking sensation of remorse settling in the pit of his stomach, Buck holstered his gun and, with Charlie Powell and Kenny Shepard, approached the motionless body of the volunteer fire chief. Together, they stood and stared down at him, bewildered at the final outcome of the horrible ordeal.

"So, he wasn't saying 'burning bridges' after all," said the deputy. "He was saying 'burning britches'. But what the hell does that mean?"

Buck looked over at Shepard. "It means plenty... doesn't it, Kenny?"

The man's robust face turned as pale as chalk. "I don't believe it," he muttered. "You mean he kept that damned grudge, even after all these years? I mean, we were just a bunch of stupid kids back then. I'd plumb forgotten all about it."

"So had I," replied Buck. "We all had... except for the one who suffered the most."

The following night found Buck Ballard sitting alone on his front porch swing, staring out into the darkness of the autumn night. He heard the lonesome call of a whippoorwill echo from the direction of Brookhollow Road and the forlorn melody nagged at a guilty spot deep down in the lawman's soul.

The creak of the screen door drew his attention. Emily gave him a sad, little smile and joined him on the swing. She took his hand in hers and, together, they sat there in silence for a long moment.

"You shouldn't blame yourself, sweetheart," she told him gently. "You know you couldn't help what you had to do. It was unavoidable."

"I know," said Buck. "But it was such a blow, finding out that he was the one responsible. I mean, we went hunting and fishing together, for heaven's sake! And we had him over for supper more times than I can even count."

"I know it's difficult to accept, but you've got to try and deal with it. David had to deal with Tommy's death... and he's just as strong and stubborn as his old man is."

Buck squeezed Emily's hand. "Thanks for the pep talk."

They sat in silence for a long time, until Emily decided to ask the question that had bothered her all day. "Why?"

Her husband said nothing. He simply stared past the porch, into the darkness of the front yard.

"Why did he do such a horrible thing?"

Buck sighed. "You wouldn't have to ask that question if you'd been born and raised in Iver's Junction," he told her. "Since you weren't, I suppose you deserve an explanation. It started with a group of mean-spirited boys and their hatred for a boy from the wrong side of the tracks. And a mangy hound dog named Old Britches."

Emily sat there patiently, waiting for her husband to continue.

"We were all about twelve years old then. It was summertime, mid-July, I believe. I was working at my father's general store that day. He'd gone to Nashville to pick up a load of goods. I was behind the counter when Sonny came strolling down the road with that red and pink hound of his. Well, the town bullies were there at the store that day, too, sitting out on the front porch drinking sodas and eating salted peanuts. They hooted and hollered at poor Sonny when he came up, picking at him and insulting him the way they always did at school. He just ignored them and came in for a pouch of chewing tobacco for his papa and an Orange Crush for himself. Old Britches stretched out in the dust of the road, like he always did and took a quick nap in the sun.

"Well, me and Sonny got to talking about baseball and comic books and such, while those boys cooked up the nastiest prank ever thought up in Trenton County. They found a gallon can of kerosene in the storage shed out back, snuck up on that poor dog, and soaked his hindquarters with it. At first, they just intended to hurt Old Britches, which is what happened when that raw kerosene hit the hound's mangy spots. Then one of the boys took it a step further and set a lit match to the howling dog. Britches went up like a bonfire. By the time Sonny and I got outside, the dog was running up and down the road like a damned fireball, while those bastards stood there and laughed their damn fool heads off. Poor Sonny couldn't do anything about it. He just chased Britches, screaming like a maniac.

"Finally, I grabbed a sack of fertilizer off the porch and ran out there, but it was too late. Old Britches had dropped in his tracks and he was just a blazing hunk of meat and not much more. I sliced open that manure sack with my jack knife and dumped it on the dog, putting out the fire. Those sons of bitches just laughed it up as they headed for town, leaving poor Sonny crying over the body of his best friend."

"That's horrible," said Emily, shaking her head. "And those boys were—?"

"Bubba McGill, Rollie Baker, Joe Cochran, and Kenny Shepard," said Buck. The sheriff chuckled humorlessly. "Funny. Kenny was the one who set Old Britches on fire and he ended up being the only one of the four who survived."

An awkward silence hung between husband and wife for a while, then Emily stood and crossed her arms against the evening chill. "It's getting late. I think I'll turn in. Coming?"

"I'll be in later," said Buck. "And thanks... for letting me tell the story."

She nodded, then disappeared through the front door.

Buck sat there until well after midnight. He thought of the little, rural town of Iver's Junction and the friends and neighbors that he knew... but did not truly know at all. He thought of hatred and fire and smoldering black death. But most of all, he thought of Sonny Bumpus.

And he wondered if there were other bad things in Trenton County that had been wrongfully forgotten during the passage of time. Things stored away and festering in someone's hidden heart.

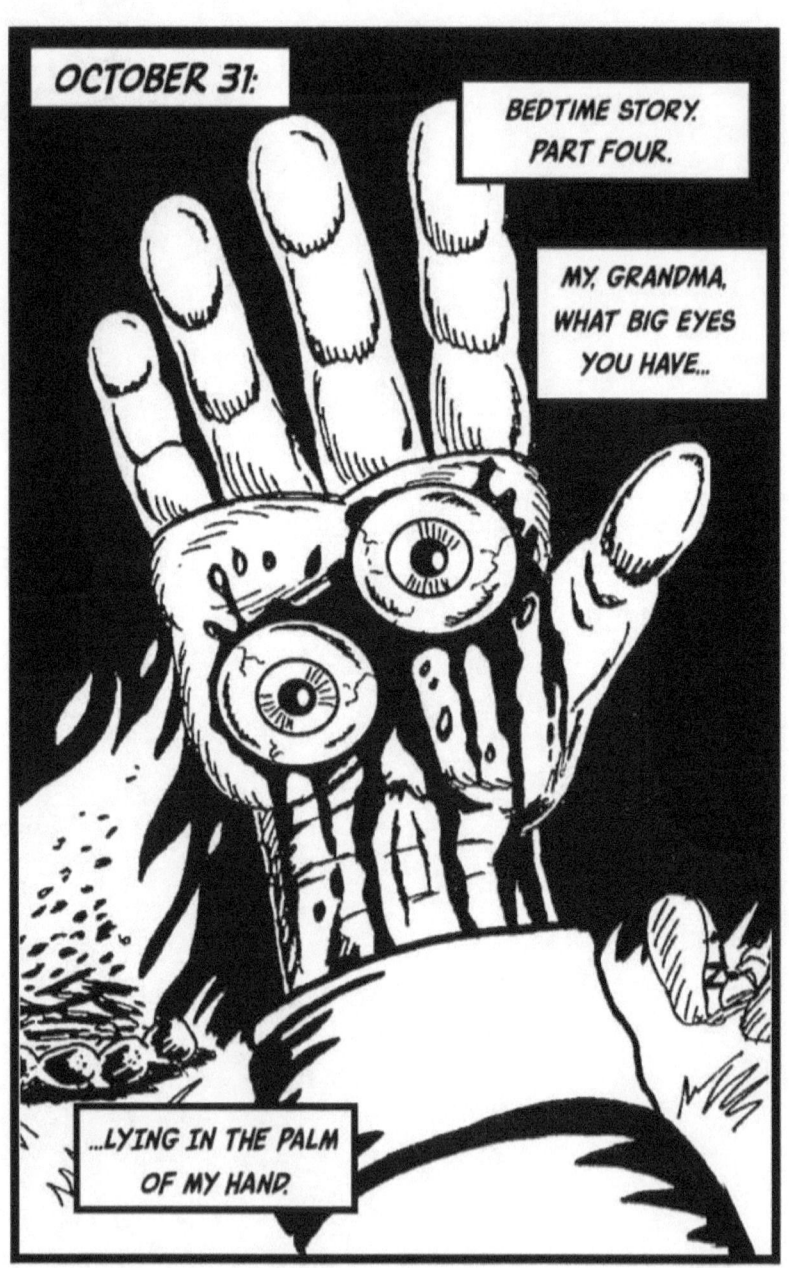

DIARY

August 21

They want to know why I killed those people in Tennessee. They want to know why a no-account bum like Jacob Weller crossed paths with the All-American family and systematically tortured, raped, and slaughtered them, one by one.

They seem very insistent for answers. But I give them none. I only counter their questions with questions of my own.

Why did Satan drive me to commit such atrocities?

Why did God allow such atrocities to take place?

They think they have me pegged. They brand me a violent psychopath and spout their psychiatric crap, but they're still missing the point. If they weren't so damned stupid, they would be able to look into my eyes and see the squirming, maggot-infested soul that lies decaying within.

You see, perversity is my forte.

It is normality that drives me insane.

August 29

My parents didn't tell me for a very long time that I once had a twin brother. When they did, they only said that he had died shortly after birth. I knew they were concealing all the gory details. Eventually, they told me the whole story... and, boy, was it a doozy!

It seems that there were once twin brothers named Jacob and Jamie. Shortly after their arrival home from the hospital, Mom and Dad went out for a night on the town, leaving the little ones in the care of teenaged babysitter Caroline. An hour later, Caroline's beatnik boyfriend, Rodney, showed up with a big bag of goodies. There was much drinking and pot smoking and airplane glue sniffing. Soon,

Caroline and Rodney had gotten wildly high and thought it would be incredibly funny to put little Jamie in the kitchen oven. They chug-a-lugged vodka and reds as they turned the flame to the max and cooked the squalling infant like a meatloaf.

Supposedly, I witnessed the whole thing, but I don't remember. Hell, I was only three months old at the time.

Those freaking junkheads had the right idea, but they made one mistake.

They baked the wrong gingerbread boy.

September 5

How about a nice bedtime story?

Once upon a time there was a clean-cut, All-American family. They never fought with one another, they attended church regularly, and lived by the Golden Rule. They lived in a cozy, suburban home, drove a minivan, and sent their children to public school... just like those perfect television families of the fifties and sixties—the Nelsons, the Cleavers, the Brady Bunch.

One summer, this family decided to take a trip to Smoky Mountain National Park. They took snapshots of the sights, watched the Cherokee Indians do their rain dance, and found a secluded campsite so they could commune with nature and enjoy the great outdoors. They sang songs, roasted marshmallows over the campfire, and swapped ghost stories. They had a wonderful time.

Then the man showed up out of nowhere, wearing a friendly smile and a stolen park ranger's uniform.

September 12

When I was six years old, I would visit my grandmother. She had this sweet, little canary named Penny. Penny would fly right out of its cage in the corner of Grandmother's sewing room and land in the palm of your hand. It would sit perfectly still and sing you the most beautiful song.

One day, while Grandmother was out working in her flower garden, I slipped into the sewing room and opened Penny's door. It flew out of its cage and lit lightly in my hand.

"Sing me a song, Penny," I said, but it remained silent.

I took a straight pin from Grandmother's sewing basket and

shoved it into Penny's little, black eye. It pierced the bird's tiny brain and emerged out the other side.

Penny sang me a song then, a very loud and frantic song... but not for very long.

September 23

Bedtime story. Part Two.
The park ranger said hello, sat down beside the fire, and drank a cup of coffee offered to him. As pleasant conversation was exchanged, he studied the All-American family. Father, mother, gray-haired grandmother, and two children, a boy and a girl. He enjoyed their company for a while, as long as he could possibly stand it. And then that damned urge crept into his demented mind...

October 7

They sent me to reform school when I was seventeen for cutting off my girlfriend's breasts with a pocketknife. After all these years, I still haven't figured out what my true motive had been. Maybe someday I'll call her up at the state asylum and ask her if she remembers why I did such a horrible thing.

October 14

Bedtime story. Part Three.
Father went first.
The friendly park ranger took a hunting knife from his belt and, with an upward thrust, drove the point up under Father's jaw. The razor-honed blade sliced effortlessly up through his tongue, the roof of his mouth, and into his tender brain. He fell forward into the campfire and burnt his face off while the ranger rounded up the rest of the All-American family...

October 19

My attorney wanted me to go for an insanity plea. I fired him and got myself another lawyer with a less attractive track record.

I keep telling them what I want, but they don't seem to take me seriously.

I want to fry.

I want the juice to surge through my body until my veins pop and I begin to sizzle like a slab of raw meat on a hot griddle.

October 31

Bedtime story. Part Four.

My, Grandma, what big eyes you have... lying in the palm of my hand.

November 4

Boy, do I miss Nam. Sometimes I cry myself to sleep, I miss it so.

I volunteered to go, you know. Not because I was patriotic, but because I heard there was a lot of weird shit going on over there. Some of the other grunts thought I was nuts for signing up, but they didn't understand. They all hated Nam, while, for me, it was pure paradise.

The first day there, the platoon sergeant took us cherries out behind a Quonset hut. There were four dead gooks lying in a ditch, riddled with bullet holes and flies. The sarge made us get down into that ditch and kick them in the head. He said it was to drive the squeamishness out of our systems before he turned us loose in the jungle. He made us kick and kick and kick until their skulls split open and their brains covered our combat boots.

Some of the guys puked their pussy guts up. I would have been down in that ditch all day if they hadn't pulled me out.

Be all that you can be...

November 8

Yesterday, some big guy named Alfonso tried to pull a caboose on me in the jailhouse showers. I was all lathered up and too fast for him, though. I backed him into a corner and, finding him to be an attentive audience, did one of my favorite impressions to entertain the sonuvabitch.

By the time the guards got there, poor Alfonso was lying on the wet tiles of the shower stall, clutching at himself as he bled to death. Me, I just stood there and watched with a bloodstained smile as they searched for the missing part of Alfonso's anatomy... one that they will never find.

You know, I do a lot of neat impressions—Bogart, Cagney... the Donner Party.

November 11

Bedtime story. Part Five.

Hey, kids, let's pretend that it's Christmas time!

That pine tree over there can be the Christmas tree and we can decorate it, too... with pieces of dear, old Mom.

We can use her fingers for tinsel and her organs for ornaments. It'll be lots of fun, just you wait and see.

Deck the halls with bowels of Mommy...

November 28

After coming back to the World, I spent some time in Mexico, smuggling drugs and wetbacks across the border. The money was good and kept me in tequila and cheap whores. Then I met up with this guy and we started making movies.

We would lure some chick off the street and take her back to our motel room. We would get her half drunk and give her a snort of coke laced with Spanish Fly. By the time my partner had his camera set up, she would be hot and ready.

Then I would come out of the bathroom, naked except for one of those weird, leather bondage masks. I would then proceed to make love to her. When she opened her mouth to scream in ecstasy, I would take the linoleum knife and, reaching between our heaving bodies...

I had that snuff film stashed somewhere in my van with all my other scrapbooks and trophies, but I didn't have an 8mm projector to watch it with. I once considered taking it to a Fotomat to have it transferred to DVD... but I chickened out at the last moment.

December 1

Bedtime story. Part Six.

How about a nursery rhyme for the children?

This little piggy went to the market.

SNAP!

This little piggy stayed home.

CRACK!

This little piggy ate roast beef.
SNAP! CRACKLE! POP!

December 13

I robbed a gas station in Tucson once and made the attendant eat a turd out of the men's room toilet, promising to spare his miserable life if he would only perform that one, simple act.

He did.

I didn't.

December 22

Bedtime story. Part Seven.

Oh, did I forget to tell you? The All-American family had a baby with them.

I was going to let it live, honest I was. But then I figured, hey, what kind of life is the kid going to have if I do? He will probably be shuffled off to some sleazy orphanage and be adopted by sadistic parents who will beat and abuse him and he will grow up to be a sick bastard… just like me.

So, I took him down to the campground trash cans and left him there.

You know, where all the hungry bears hang out for breakfast.

January 7

Well, it's official now. The jury handed down their verdict and the trial is over. The death penalty. I get off just thinking about it.

In some states it is lethal injection, in others the gas chamber. Here in Tennessee it is Old Sparky… the tried-and-true electric chair.

As for my journal, this will be the last entry. The wire that I pried from the springs of my bunk is getting dull and the words are barely legible now. For, you see, the exploits I have penned have not been committed to paper… but to human flesh. I am a living tome; all my sins and atrocities have been carved into every inch of skin, or at least the places that I could reach.

Perhaps, following my execution, the grisly accounts of my life's work will be made public. Perhaps some unscrupulous individual will bribe a morgue attendant into letting them take photos of my body and they will end up in a sleazy tabloid or on some offbeat website. Then all the world will be privy to my pursuit of barbarity and perversion.

So, if you are browsing the internet during the late hours of the night, and come upon me... please, indulge your morbid curiosity.

Come... read my diary.

FLUID

"You could catch a staph infection just *breathing* in here," Sandra Horton told herself as she attempted to wash her hands while touching the grungy spigots of the ladies' room sink as sparingly as possible.

The gas station was a cubbyhole of filth and neglect. It appeared that the proprietor had failed to give the restroom a thorough scrubbing for at least a couple of years. It stank of mildew, used sanitary pads, and stale urine. The men's room was undoubtedly in the same sorry condition, she concluded, probably with the crowning addition of cigarette butt-clogged urinal and an ancient condom dispenser that offered the interstate truckers the foil-wrapped promise of protection and a good time for a mere three bucks.

The mirror over the sink was dirty and sported a couple of garish pink lip imprints where someone had blotted their lipstick against the cloudy surface. As Sandra looked at them, they blazed as bright and jarring as neon against her retinas. Immediately, she closed her eyes. *Just do like the doctors told you*, she thought. *Shut your eyes and relax, and it'll just go away.*

When she opened her eyes again, the unnatural Day-Glo pink had faded to its normal, muted shade.

The warm Tennessee sunshine embraced her as she stepped outside, driving the unclean horror—and the overly brilliant lip prints—from her mind. After all, this was supposed to be a vacation, a time for fun and relaxation, and not for getting uptight over petty annoyances. For Sandra, it was also a time of long overdue triumph and thumbing her nose at her traitorous jerk of an ex-husband, Michael.

Yes, the past two years had been difficult and even unbearable at times, enduring the awful bouts of depression and disorientation, locked up in that special "resort", as her psychiatrist liked to phrase it. And, most of all, being deprived of her children, Joey and Tina, and her God-given right of motherhood.

The labels they had branded her with had been unnecessary and cruel. Manic depressive, paranoid schizophrenic, and several more she had never heard of or was even able to pronounce. They said that she was grossly "overprotective" of her children, that she "jumped to conclusions" and "made mountains out of molehills". She couldn't believe they would inflict such mean-spirited lies upon her, even after those two *minor* incidents. Sure, maybe she overreacted a little, chopping up the neighbor's dog with a garden hoe after it had torn the cuff of Joey's new jeans. But the incident concerning the homeless man by the schoolyard had been perfectly justified in her mind; the natural reaction of a mother protecting her child. How was she to know what his intentions were when she had arrived to pick up her children and found the man speaking to Tina through the chain-link fence? How could she have possibly known he was only asking directions to the rescue mission a couple of blocks away? He could have just as easily been some perverted pedophile, rather than a man down on his luck. Besides, she hadn't even killed him when she jumped curb and ran him down with the family car. Nothing serious… just a concussion and a few broken bones.

And then there was the matter of her frustrating vision anomaly. A one-in-a-million defect of the optical nerve that cranked the color spectrum to the max at any given moment, causing lemon yellow to seem as bright and blinding as the sun, and black as dark and depthless as a bottomless well. She recalled the neon lips and shook her head. Just a damn annoyance, that was all. Nothing to worry about. It freaked her out sometimes, but she could handle it.

Anyway, all of that—the accusations and distrust—was behind her now. Due to months of therapy and a strict regimen of medication, Sandra had realized and accepted her obsessive behavior, as well as the reason for her bouts of overstimulated color attacks. Even after her release, it had taken nearly a year of hearings and legal action to simply gain minimal visitation privileges. This past weekend, for instance. Sandra was only supposed to have the kids for an afternoon of shopping at the local mall. Instead, she had suggested that she, Joey, Tina, and the family dog, Sport, hop in the car and head to Florida. The children had been reluctant at first, but she had convinced them that the only reason Dad hadn't told them about the trip was to keep it a special surprise.

It was Wednesday morning now, and as it turned out, the

whimsical trip had been a glorious success. They had spent most of their time on the beach in Saint Petersburg and had a wonderful time, she and her darling youngsters. The only one who undoubtedly *wasn't* enjoying himself was her backstabbing ex. Michael would be pulling his hair in worry and fear, agonizing over the whereabouts of *his* precious children, wondering if Schizoid Sandra had absconded with them to some foreign country where American law had no say-so over custody matters.

Let him sweat, she thought with a grin. She walked down a narrow sidewalk along the whitewashed wall of the gas station office. *Let him suffer a little mental anguish for a change. He deserves it after all he's put me through!*

Turning the corner, she nearly ran into a lanky farmer-type, wearing bib overalls and a John Deere cap. For a moment she looked into his weathered face and was stricken by his eyes. The irises glowed an eerie green, like something lit up by one of those black light lamps of her youth. *He's an alien!* her mind screamed, and that familiar rush of panic threatened to overtake her. As the man nodded politely, she stopped, shut her eyes, and breathed deep. When she opened her eyes, she found that the blazing green had been replaced by a natural hazel hue.

"Are you okay, ma'am?" the farmer asked with concern.

"Of course," she said, rushing past him. "I'm fine!"

The only reason they had stopped in the rural town in the first place, instead of driving straight through to Louisville, was because of the damned car. It had been acting up all during their stay in Florida, the transmission jerking and slipping with annoying frequency. So, she had decided to have it checked before they became stranded on the long stretch of interstate. The Tennessee town boasted a gas station as well as a small strip mall, a grocery store, a rent-to-own furniture store, and a Dairy Queen.

After having the tank filled to capacity, Sandra had conceded to letting the owner/mechanic of the hayseed pit stop take a look under the good. "Just pull 'er into the second bay over yonder and I'll check 'er out," the attendant in the greasy gray coveralls had said, grinning, eying her trim figure with undisguised interest.

Sandra had done as he requested and then retired to the restroom to freshen up a bit. She had instructed the kids to stay put in the front office and warned them not to speak to the redneck mechanic while he took a look beneath the hood.

She now sidestepped a rack of bargain retreads and walked into the cramped office. "Alright, you two, if you need to go pee before we leave, you'd better do it now. And don't touch anything you don't have to. This place is absolutely filthy!"

But her words were wasted, for there was no one there in the cluttered room with its overpriced fan belts, hula girl air fresheners, and sun-yellowed road maps. The children were nowhere to be found. The only one there was Sport, the kids' Golden Retriever. He lay, head on paws, beside an antique rolltop desk covered with FRAM, STP, and NASCAR stickers.

"Those blasted kids!" she grumbled in irritation. "I told them to stay put." She crouched to scratch the dog behind his shaggy ears. "Did they desert you, boy? Did they leave you all alone?"

Toby only whined and cringed at her touch, as if he was scared half out of his wits.

"What's the matter?" she asked, then let her words trail off. She withdrew her hand from the dog's matted fur. Her palm was covered with something very wet and sticky. Something starkly crimson in color.

"What's wrong, Sport?" she asked, shocked. Uneasiness began to well up inside her. "Did you hurt yourself?" She checked him thoroughly but found no wound... only that bright red splotch of sticky fluid on his head and upper back.

Sandra stood and, with a cold stone of dread settling in the pit of her stomach, walked to the door leading into the three-bay garage.

"Joey... Tina... kids, are you out there?"

She received no reply.

Sport hung at her heels, whimpering, as she made her way across the oil-stained concrete floor. The only car in the garage was her own, the old Ford station wagon with the oxidized silver paint job. She could hear the quiet sounds of tinkering near the exposed engine, the open hood obscuring the view of the man who worked there. She expected to hear the giggles and annoying questions of her children drift from that direction, but they didn't. The only other sound was that of the mechanic himself, whistling an off-key rendition of an old Johnny Cash tune.

She opened her mouth to call to her kids again, when she noticed the splash of bright crimson on the left rear door of the car. It ran in thick, tacky streamlets from the open window, down the curve of the door, to pool in a damp puddle underneath.

Oh God! she thought to herself. *What is this? What on earth happened?*

Creeping forward, inch by torturous inch, Sandra peered into the back seat. The gray upholstery was saturated with the sticky red liquid. Tina's stuffed dolphin she had purchased at a souvenir shop lay in the puddle of congealing substance, the staring white eyes now dyed a brilliant blood red.

She nearly screamed when the mechanic stepped around the front fender of the car, wiping his huge hands on a blue shop rag. He grinned with the swagger of a redneck who thought he was God's gift to women. Usually, such an attitude would have infuriated Sandra, but at that moment horror was the only thing that seized her thoughts. The front of the man's filthy coveralls was covered with rosy redness.

He smiled broadly, a toothpick protruding from one corner of his mouth. "Oh, I found that little problem of yours, lady. Nothing serious really, just the..."

"What have you done?" she managed, jumping backward.

The grease monkey looked convincingly puzzled at first. "Pardon me?" Then he saw that she had noticed the ugly mess on and inside her car. Sandra watched his eyes narrow a degree as he attempted to cook up a suitable explanation. "Aw, shucks, ma'am, I'm mighty sorry about that. You see, your dog tripped me up and made me..."

"My children! *Where are my children?*"

The mechanic, whose embroidered uniform patch identified him as BUD, cast his eyes curiously around the shadowy garage. "Gee, I don't know. I could've sworn they were right here a moment ago."

"WHAT HAVE YOU DONE TO MY CHILDREN!!" Sandra demanded. She began to slowly back away from the big man with the gore-stained uniform.

She watched as Bud's true colors began to bleed through. His beefy face flushed with sudden anger. "Now, you just wait one minute, lady! I ain't done nothing to your..."

"YOU'VE MURDERED THEM, HAVEN'T YOU?" screamed the woman. "YOU'VE KILLED THEM, YOU BASTARD! SLAUGHTERED THEM! JUST LOOK AT THE BLOOD... *THEIR* BLOOD!"

A strange expression crossed the mechanic's face. His anger disappeared and was replaced by another, less defined emotion. He started forward, his hands outstretched. Perhaps he was advancing to comfort her, to soothe her mistaken notions. But, then again, perhaps he was coming to silence her as he had silenced Joey and Tina. Sandra was unable to determine what the man's true intentions were.

She didn't wait to find out. Feeling on the cluttered workbench behind her, she discovered something heavy and blunt. She clutched it tightly in her trembling hand, then swung it over her shoulder with all her strength. The intended target was Bud's nose. It snapped loudly with an explosion of blood as the monkey wrench completed its downward swipe.

"Dammit, woman, what the hell are you...?"

She surged forward, her terror providing the necessary momentum as she swung again and again. The heavy wrench eluded Bud's feeble attempts at self-protection, clubbing him across the face and head, splitting flesh, shattering teeth, battering and bruising.

"Stop it... you crazy bitch... stop it or I'll..."

"YOU FIEND!" shrieked Sandra, knocking him to his back with a particularly vicious strike. The adjustable jaws of the tool came away matted with blood, flesh, and hair. "YOU KILLED THEM! YOU KILLED MY BABIES!"

"No... don't. Please... stop it..."

Her blows punctuated each shrill word of accusation. "KILLED THEM... YOU... LOUSY... SON OF A... BITCH!"

Finally, the aching of her lean arms and the force of her sobbing caused her to stop. The mechanic lay moaning in the empty space of the first garage bay, cussing and spitting and sputtering on his own blood. His face was swollen, gory mask, the face of a monster and no longer that of the good-natured clown who had seduced her youngsters toward the brink of unsuspecting butchery.

Sandra stumbled to the far wall, feeling as if she might vomit. A girlie calendar featuring a big-breasted blonde hung on the greasy cinderblock wall, and beside it, something else. It was a wall winch with a jutting handle and a length of heavy chain stretching up and over a pulley in the ceiling. She followed the chain with her eyes. Dangling from the opposite end—directly above the injured man— was a very greasy, very heavy-appearing engine block.

Bud began to swear, trying desperately to lift himself, but too weak to do so. "Get the hell away from that, lady... please, just step away..."

Sandra watched the big man lying there, pleading and groveling, glaring at her with a mixture of fear and panic. All she could do was laugh at his petty attempts to save his own life. With a snarling expression of intense satisfaction, Sandra reached over, took hold of the rubber-coated handle, and disengaged the winch lock.

The block fell like the blade of a guillotine. Bud opened his mouth to scream, but all that escaped was a wet wheeze as the engine bore down on his chest, caving in his ribcage, crushing him instantly like a bug underfoot. There were a few spasmodic shudders, then his limbs grew deathly still.

Sandra let the monkey wrench drop from her hand. It hit the concrete floor with a resounding *clang*. Sport whimpered and nudged at her blue-jeaned hip. She crouched to hug him, tears streaming down her blood-speckled cheeks.

"I got him, boy," she wept. "I got the murdering bastard."

Then, from the open garage door, came a child's voice.

"Mom?"

Sandra spun, heart pounding, mind racing toward the breaking point, as she rose and stared at…

… the two children, brother and sister, melting ice cream cones in hand, their faces pale and confused as they stared at…

… the prone body of a small-town garage mechanic known simply as Bud, his broad chest sunken beneath five hundred pounds of cast iron and steel, his swollen eyes surprised but unseeing, as he stared dully at…

… the gallon container of spilt transmission fluid sitting on the fender of Sandra's car, dribbling streams of sticky redness, which, upon closer inspection, really didn't look that much like human blood at all.

TRAPS

Jerry Hoffman loved his wife.

They had been high school sweethearts back in '84. He had bent down to retrieve a pencil she had dropped, and their eyes had locked when he handed it back. Joe remembered that jolt of electricity that had passed between them, more than attraction or even anything sexual. They both had known it was love at first sight. That electricity had lasted for a long time; during their dating, their first year of marriage, even while raising Jack and Kimberly. It was a love he thought would never change... would never grow old or stale or questionable.

Jerry Hoffman loved his job.

Some people looked down their noses at what he did daily, and sometimes on the weekends if necessary. Some people even laughed at it (his snobby in-laws included), even though it was a service that was necessary and made people's lives better and less uncomfortable. Joe loved helping animals. He loved taking them out of bad situations and putting them where they belonged. Where they could be free and live the way nature intended them to be.

But Jerry Hoffman also hated some things.

He hated lying and deceit. He hated texting and calling and receiving no answer, even though he knew a phone was within reach. He hated looking into someone's eyes—someone he still loved deeply— and seeing an emptiness that was both saddening and frightful. He hated having his emotions trifled with. He hated for someone to wad them up in a ball like a piece of worthless paper to be tossed into the trash... or flushed down a toilet like an insignificant turd.

And, most of all, Jerry Hoffman hated traps.

Monday afternoon he went beneath the Baxters' house with a job to do.

Jerry was tall, but lean. He could fit in the tightest crawlspace and maneuver well. Once inside, he paused and closed his eyes. Smelled the dankness of earth and heard the sounds common of such places—the muffling of voices above him, the creaking of floorboards, the gurgle of water through PCV pipe. When he detected the sound that wasn't common—a metallic rattling and a shrill squeaking—he opened his eyes and turned on the little halogen light he wore above the bill of his baseball cap, the cap that read Anytime Extermination & Pest Retrieval Service. Then he headed toward the far northeastern corner of the foundation.

He was surprised to find two in the cage. Two rather large rats with coarse gray fur and pink tails whipping nervously back and forth. The rodents were agitated. Jerry could see the fear in their beady eyes, and a healthy dose of malice. If he had stuck a finger through the wire mesh, they would have taken a chunk clean out of it. They had been in there for a while. Droppings littered the floor of the cage, and the odor of urine was strong and acidic in his nostrils.

Jerry couldn't help but chuckle. The sound seemed to piss them off. They paced back and forth in the eight-by-twelve-inch trap. "We got the big boys here," he said with a grin of admiration. "No puny little field mice. Genuine *rattus norvegicus.*"

The rats glared at him and hissed. They were hungry, that was for sure, practically starved. Probably hadn't had a bite for a day, maybe more. They would have probably attacked and eaten one another, if he hadn't shown up to prevent it.

He backed out of the crawlspace, taking the trap with him. Once outside, Joe dusted himself off and turned off the little light on his cap. He knocked on the back door and, when the lady of the house answered, he lifted the cage to present his findings. Mrs. Baxter recoiled in disgust. "Good Lord! Did you get them all?"

"Hopefully," he said, handing her a handwritten invoice for the service. "But if you start hearing scratching or gnawing again, give me a call and I'll bring another trap."

She ducked inside the house, hurriedly wrote him a check, and handed it to him past the screen door. "Where did they come from? This is a nice neighborhood."

"That it is, Mrs. Baxter," Jerry told her. "But the county dump is half a mile down the road and a few probably wandered down here, looking for greener pastures."

A moment later, he opened the rear of his van and set the cage inside. It wasn't the only receptacle in the vehicle. There was a glass box with a nest of scorpions—Centruoides vittatus or the striped bark scorpion—he had dug from a stack of rotten boards at Jenson's Lumberyard, and a narrow wooden crate containing a good-sized western diamondback, *Crotalus atrox*, that Jerry had captured on the walking track near Trinity University.

The lanky man took a handkerchief from his hip pocket and mopped his brow. The Texas sun was hot and merciless that day. "Brought y'all some company," he told the other captives. "Be civil and play nice. Plenty of time to raise hell later."

Closing the double doors, he climbed into the van and headed for his next stop of the day.

Jerry Hoffman hated traps… but sometimes they were necessary.

That night, Jerry sat at the kitchen table and ate a hamburger he'd bought at a greasy spoon on his way home from work. He washed it down with a Corona and stared at his cell phone. He wanted to pick it up and put it to use… wanted to make the call. But he knew what that would get him.

Of course, Elaine wasn't there. She was away on one of her trips… with Kyle.

"It'll only be a week and a half," she had told him. "Kyle wants to make sure the new plant gets off to a smooth start. Come on, he *is* my boss. I can't let him down. Besides, it's good money. He's paying me time and half the entire trip."

Jerry knew that she was telling the truth. Kyle Andrews was opening another aluminum recycling plant, his third, in Atlanta.

But it was what Elaine and Kyle were doing after hours that weighed heavily on his mind. He picked up the phone and turned it on. *Leave it be*, he told himself, *you're just gonna feel like shit afterward. Like you always do.*

But he couldn't help it. Jerry found her name in his contacts and pressed it. It rang half a dozen times before she answered. He was surprised that she even made the effort.

"Hello?" Elaine's voice sounded winded, like she was out of breath.

"Hey, hon," he said, taking another swallow of beer. "It's me."

"Jerry… what do you need? You woke me up, sweetheart. We had a long day at the plant. I turned in about eight."

"Sorry," he told her, although he wasn't sorry at all. "Just wanted to make sure when you'll be coming home."

There was a long stretch of silence. Well, not precisely silence… more like a muffled pause, like a hand was trying to block him from hearing what was going on a thousand miles away. He strained his ears and scarcely heard a man's laugh and her whisper, *"Stop it! Behave yourself!"* Then her voice was back, irritated. "I told you before, we're flying back in on Sunday night."

"Okay," said Jerry. "Just wanted to make sure." He hesitated. *Don't say it*, he warned himself, but he did anyway. "I love you."

"Yeah. Well, I better get back to sleep." Then the phone was silent, and she was gone.

Jerry stared at his burger but didn't finish it. It had suddenly soured in his stomach. He stood up and, taking his beer with him, left the kitchen, then walked down the hallway to his bedroom.

He turned on the light. There was a dresser with a mirror to one side and a chest-of-drawers on the other, but the piece of furniture that dominated the room—and had the entire twenty-five years of their marriage—was the bed. That big king-sized bed with the ornate brass head and footboards and posts a good six feet high, with shiny brass knobs at the top.

Jerry sat down on Elaine's cedar chest and sipped his beer. He sat there for a long time, just staring at the bed.

It had been between those four posts that everything had gone to hell. Oh, not at first. At the beginning, the bed had been heaven on earth. Lord have mercy, Elaine could give a bed—and a man—a workout, especially when she was a younger woman. At first, she had used it for sleeping and lovemaking, for conceiving their young'uns… then, later, for other things.

If you love me, you'll get me a...
The list had been long and plentiful, and the request always punctuated with an orgasm that would jar the fillings from your teeth. *A new dress... a diamond ring... a new car... a cruise to the Bahamas... a boob job.* That last one had excited him at first, especially since she was flatter than roadkill armadillo on a sunbaked highway. But after she got them, the sex had diminished and the distance between him and her had broadened. The sheets of the big bed had grown cool and untangled, and the brass frame had ceased its squeak and rattle. Elaine started working for Kyle and began putting her new assets to work in ways that benefited her and her only.

Jerry drained the beer bottle and wished he had brought another with him. He sat there for a long time, alone with his thoughts. His children were grown and gone, and his wife was three states away, balling her boss. He was in the house all alone... just him and the bed.

Jerry Hoffman hated traps. Especially beautiful, shiny ones that ensnared one's heart and soul, like a spider's web entangling a fly in its sticky strands.

The following day started with—could you believe it—spiders.

Jerry extracted a nest of black widows from beneath a playground slide at Apache Creek Park, then picked up several small plastic traps bearing brown recluse spiders from the storage room of a Burger King in Alamo Heights. He assured his clients that he would promptly dispose of the arachnids. But when he returned to his van, he placed them in a Rubbermaid tote for safekeeping.

After that, he drove fifteen miles south of San Antonio to the outlying community of Pearsall. The Friday before, he had set up a bat box in the loft of a horse stable a short distance off Highway 81. Before climbing to the loft, Jerry donned Kevlar sleeves and heavy leather gloves, to avoid getting scratched or bitten. When he opened the box, he discovered seven brown bats, *myotis lucifugus*, clinging to the inner walls. He suspected, from their behavior and the gummy secretions from their nostrils and mouths, that all seven could very well be rabid.

The remainder of his day consisted of rounding up more of the usual suspects: rats, rattlesnakes, scorpions, as well as a couple of Gila monsters that had scared an old lady in her cactus garden over in Gardendale. And there had been a wasp nest the size of a basketball in the attic of a Baptist church in Leon Valley, teaming with temperamental *polistes carolina*. Jerry handled each case with the utmost care and precision, avoiding potential chaos and dispatching them to his van... all alive and thoroughly pissed off about being extracted from the respective homes.

Jerry Hoffman hated traps... but sometimes they could be productive and fruitful.

That night, after supper, Jerry took a walk around the old single-level house that he had lived in for the past thirty-three years.

First, he observed the bedroom. He stood at the foot of the big brass bed, then walked from one side to the other. The floor creaked beneath his work boots at certain points and he took mental note of those particular locations. Other spots seemed sturdy, with no give to them at all. It was those places that worried him the most.

Secondly, he walked down the hallway, past the kitchen, and into the utility room. Between the washer and dryer, there was a narrow door. Jerry opened it and stared down into the darkness of the cellar beneath the house. He reached up and fumbled until he found the pull-chain of an overhead light. A sixty-watt bulb snapped on, bathing steep stairs in a pale, yellow glow.

Jerry descended the stairs and reached the concrete floor of the basement. Shelves of junk, laden with dust and laced with cobwebs, lined the cinderblock walls. He walked to the far end of the cellar and stood directly beneath a certain point, staring up at the rafters and the boards of the ceiling just above. He knew beyond those boards was a blanket of pink insulation and, a few inches further, the floorboards of an upper room.

He studied a support beam that traveled from floor to ceiling, then reached out and gave it a tug. It held fast but creaked a little...

not as sturdy as he originally thought. He found three others and tested them as well. Satisfied, he walked across the cellar to the back of the foundation. He reached up and unfastened a narrow window, allowing it to swing inward on its hinges. Beyond, the Texas night was dark, cool, and strangely silent. Not one cricket made itself known. Twenty yards from the basement window, Jerry could barely make out the pale structure of the storage building at the far end of his property.

Satisfied, he mounted the stairs and, reaching the top, turned the cellar light off with a jerk of the chain.

Jerry Hoffman hated traps… but if a man was to construct one successfully, he had to put a little thought and nerve into its completion and eventual execution.

"You wanted to see me, Mr. Gonzalez?"

"Come in, Hoffman," his boss said from behind his desk.

Almost timidly, Jerry stepped into his superior's office. Self-consciously, he removed his cap and held it in his hands before him.

"Shut the door and sit down, please."

Jerry did as he was told. He waited almost a full minute before the man spoke.

"You didn't turn in your monthly objective log, Mr. Hoffman. In fact, you didn't turn one in last month either. Do you remember us having a conversation concerning that discrepancy a few weeks ago?"

"Objective" log. That was what Luis Gonzalez called the pests they captured and killed… *objectives*. "Yes, sir. I remember."

"Then why do you continue to ignore company policy?" Gonzalez asked him. "You know that it is a requirement of your position with Anytime EPRS to keep accurate records of the objectives you have captured and disposed of. Not only are your records inaccurate, but they are non-existent."

"I'm sorry, sir," Jerry said, although, secretly, he wasn't sorry at all. "I reckon I just get so busy that I forget to fill out the log sheets."

Gonzalez stared at him in that annoying deadpan expression

of his. "That's not acceptable, Mr. Hoffman. Not by me, our district manager, or the founder of Anytime Extermination at the corporate office in Dallas. From this moment forward, you *will* find time to accurately log your objectives and the manner of their disposal. If you continue to fall short of company expectations, we may have no other choice but to terminate your employment. Do you understand?"

Jerry nodded. "Yes, sir. I understand. Completely."

"Then you may leave and clock out for the day. And, Hoffman, I do expect a complete and accurate objective log for this month on my desk bright and early Monday morning. That would go a long way to convince me that you are a productive contributor to the Anytime team."

"Yes, sir. Monday morning."

A few minutes later, Jerry Hoffman clocked out and walked across the parking lot to his Anytime van. He couldn't help but smile to himself. He had absolutely no intention of turning in an accurate log of the pests he had exterminated... for the simple fact that he had no such information to share.

Before reaching the vehicle, he considered Gonzalez and the ass-chewing he had just received from him. Jerry also considered leaving a nasty surprise on the floorboard of the man's Lexus, but knew that restraint was crucial that Friday afternoon.

Jerry Hoffman hated traps... especially those built from rules and regulations and manned by smug assholes who had never walked in his shoes or dirtied their manicured hands with crawlspace earth or attic dust.

On Saturday night, Jerry made the call.

"Hello?" Elaine's voice sounded perpetually annoyed.

"Hey, hon. It's Jerry. I just wanted to let you know that I got a call from my sister a few minutes ago. They think Mom had a stroke. I'm gonna head up to see her... probably stay a few days until she's out of the ICU."

There was a short pause. Then Elaine replied. "You're going to drive all the way to Amarillo?" Did he detect a tone of eagerness in her voice?

"Yeah. I'm sorry I won't be here Sunday night to welcome you home. I hate you coming back to an empty house like that."

"Well, that's okay, sweetheart. It's your mother, after all. You should be there for her."

Jerry grinned sourly and shook his head. Elaine absolutely hated his mother's guts. Hearing her speak about her with such warmth and concern told him that she had taken the bait. Hook, line, and sinker.

"By the way," he told her, "I got bored, you know, with you not being here and all, so I polished up that brass bed of yours really nice. Really put the elbow grease to it. Shines like pure gold."

"Thank you so much, darling. I really appreciate that."

He wondered if she had her phone on speaker... if *he* was privy to their conversation. He could almost sense Kyle nibbling at the bait, too, ready to bite.

"Well, you have a good rest of the evening... and a safe trip home tomorrow night. I love you." Those last three words went down like the bitterest of pills.

"And I love you, too, sweetheart. You be careful driving to Amarillo."

"I will. Good night."

Jerry ended the call. He sighed and stared at the brass bed for a long moment. Then he slipped on his denim jacket and left the house.

He opened the back doors of the Anytime van. It was empty, except for what he had purchased in town earlier that day... at Home Depot.

Then he turned to the storage shed. The double doors were heavily padlocked.

Now came the tricky part.

Jerry Hoffman hated traps... but if you wanted to catch the intended prey, a good one required teeth that would grab hold and refuse to let go. Teeth that were wickedly sharp and as tenacious as hell.

Sunday night. 8:47 pm.

Jerry parked the van behind the storage shed, out of sight. He sat behind the steering wheel, nursing his fourth beer of the evening. Waiting.

He heard the car thirty seconds before it turned in the driveway. There was the slamming of doors, a man's laughter, a woman's giggling. Faint footfalls on the front porch risers and the jingle of fumbled keys. When he heard the slam of the front door, Jerry left the van, rounded the building, and walked across the yard. He stood for a moment, a few feet from the bedroom window.

More laughter, sly and dirty. Then the urgent jouncing of bed springs.

Jerry walked back to the van and started it up. He backed the vehicle around the side of the storage shed until its rear bumper pointed toward the house. The trailer hitch had been a bitch to install... after all, he was an exterminator, not a mechanic or a handyman. He thought of Mr. Gonzalez and what he might say.

Something like "that's not a company-authorized modification, Mr. Hoffman!"

He walked to the open window of the cellar. He crouched down and lifted the four lengths of heavy chain that lay in the sun-scorched grass of the back yard. One end he secured to the hitch. The other end was unseen... obscured by the darkness of the basement, on the other side of the rectangular window.

The squeaking of the springs accompanied a symphony of carnal noises. Grunts and moans that would make a porn star blush. They were much too busy to hear Jerry stamp on the gas and send the van surging away with a lurch. Much too involved to hear the metallic clink of the four chains as they tightened... or the groan of timbers holding firm for a long moment, before splintering and giving way.

Jerry cut the engine and listened. There was a crackling of floorboards inside the house, then a horrific crash, as though the entire structure was caving in on itself.

After that, they began to scream.

Oh, how they screamed...

Calmly, Jerry climbed out of the van and walked to the back door of the house. He let himself in and walked down the hallway to the bedroom. He stood outside the door, careful not to step foot inside. Reaching in and, feeling along the wall, he located the light switch and turned it on.

The bedroom floor was gone. In its place was a deep crater of jagged boards and timbers. The bedroom's overhead light revealed what all the screaming was about.

Elaine and Kyle lay amid a tangle of bloody bed linen and twisted brass railing in the basement's pit. They thrashed wildly and screamed loudly as the "teeth" of the trap took hold and held them securely, preventing their escape.

Most folks didn't like to bring their work home with them, but Jerry had. Two months' worth... caged and starved and locked in the shed out back. Until, one by one, they had been transferred from their confinement and released into the pitch darkness of the basement. Hungry and enraged... slithering, skittering, swarming... ready to strike.

Jerry stood at the edge of the doorway and watched. Those pesky "objectives" that Mr. Gonzalez regarded so highly covered his cheating wife and her lover. Elaine lurched in agony and wailed hoarsely, her once-lovely face swelling into a mottled purple mask as wasps and scorpions sank their stingers deeply into her cheeks and forehead. Two bats, diseased and seeking sustenance, latched onto the nipples of her breasts. Spiders and centipedes clung to her abdomen, refusing to let go. The soles of her feet pressed against the sagging surface of the mattress, as though attempting to push her body into a sitting position. Instead, her legs spread, exposing a portal far too inviting to deny. A rat the size of a puppy loped across the mattress and burrowed into the tender folds of her womanhood, wiggling, burrowing, disappearing from sight.

Kyle Masters was fairing no better. His once toned and tanned physique was now covered in angry welts and open wounds where flesh had been torn away and devoured. His groin—which had been aroused and near the point of release moments before—was obscured by a tangle of slithering, biting fury. Two rattlers were fighting over the deflated column of Kyle's penis, their fangs anchored deeply, pumping ounce upon ounce of venom into his veins and capillaries. A particularly large Gila monster had its broad jaws clamped firmly on the man's testicles, crushing the organs into jelly, adding its poisonous contribution to the death that was already coursing through the bossman's bloodstream.

Before Elaine's eyes were picked away by two carrion crows, she stared up at her husband. Jerry matched her gaze until her orbs ruptured beneath darting beaks. Then he turned away and walked back down the hallway. Behind him, the shrieks and screams faded and grew quiet, replaced by the rattling of serpentine buttons, the scurrying of rodent feet, and the bat-like flapping of membrane stretched tautly from one thin bone to another.

Feeling numb and drained, he walked back to the van and slipped the chains from the trailer hitch. He started up the van and pulled out onto the highway. A mile or so away was an access road that led into the desert.

A burlap bag on the seat next to him stirred and, within, a rattle began to buzz, followed by another... and yet another.

He knew a spot twenty miles in the wilderness where no one would think of looking for him. And, if they did, it would be too late.

Once he untied that bag and unleashed what was within, he knew he would simply sit there and await his fate. He had no reason—or desire—to do otherwise.

Jerry Hoffman hated traps... especially ones that you were forced to set for yourself.

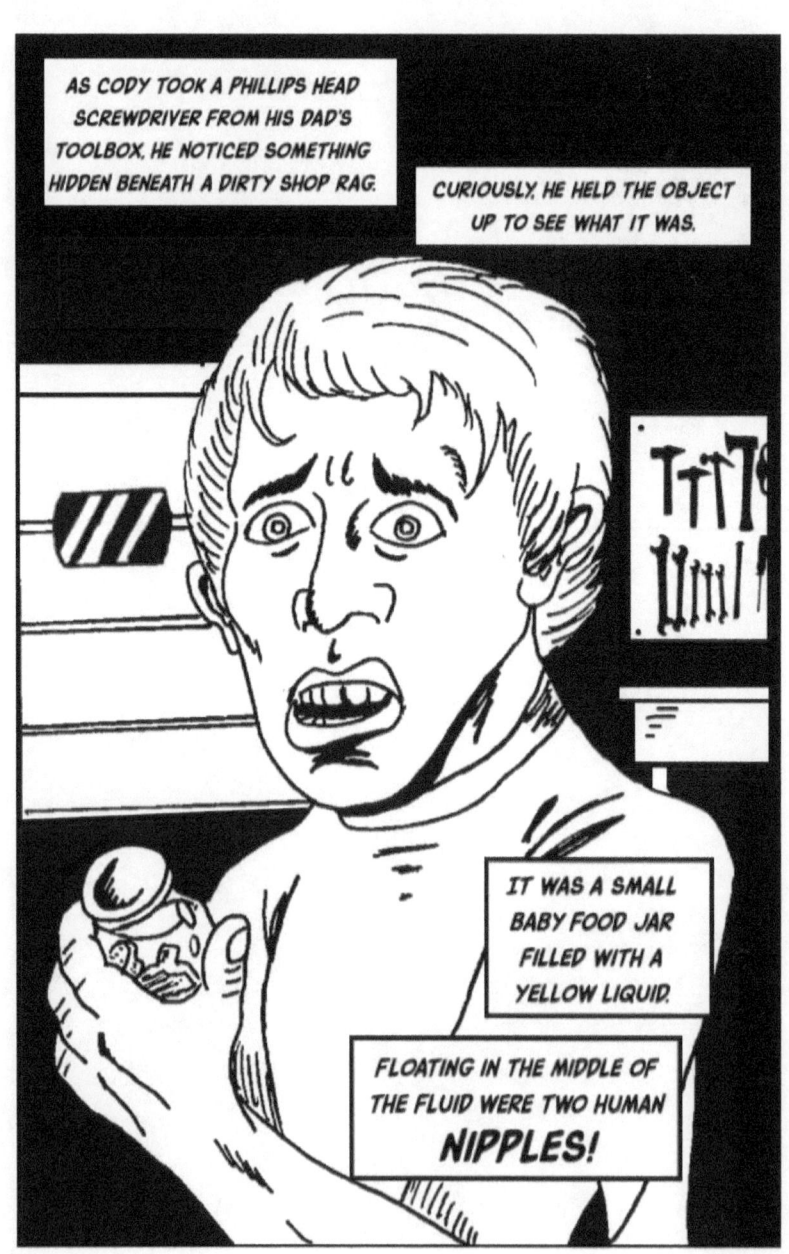

THE NIPPLES IN DAD'S TOOLBOX

It all started that morning in late July when Mom asked for a screwdriver from her junk drawer in the kitchen.

"A Phillips head, not a flat head," she emphasized. The hinges on the shower door in the bathroom adjoining her and Dad's bedroom had come loose again. She was holding onto it for dear life, hoping that she wouldn't lose her grip and drop the door into the stall. If it shattered, she would be sweeping and picking glass out of the shower for an hour or so.

Cody Dawson nodded. "Right. Phillips head." Then he was heading for the kitchen.

But when the twelve-year-old checked the top drawer next to the sink, all he found was a flat head screwdriver. "Dang!"

"Hurry up, sweetheart," called Mom from the bathroom. "This thing is heavy!"

Cody figured maybe Dad had one in the garage. This father was a mechanic down at Casey's Exxon, so he had a load of tools, at home and at work. He opened the door on the far side of the utility room and ran across the driveway to the standalone two-car garage.

Luckily, it was unlocked. His dad was funny about things like that. Kept things locked up all the time. He was a little surprised that the side door opened with no trouble at all. It was dark in there and cooler than it was outside. It reeked of oil and grease and freshly mown grass from where Dad had cut the yard yesterday evening with the riding mower. Cody felt along the wall next to the door and found the light switch.

Even with the double banks of fluorescent lights, the interior of the garage was still shadowy. He rushed over to Dad's big red, twelve-drawer tool chest—the one nearly as tall as he was—and tried each drawer, one by one. All were securely locked. Frustrated, he looked around the garage. He was about to leave when he spotted a rusty toolbox beneath the work bench against the far wall. It was nestled between an old carburetor and a gallon of 50/50 antifreeze.

Cody crouched and pulled the toolbox out into the open. *Funny... I've never seen this here before,* he thought to himself. *Maybe because I wasn't looking for it... duh!* The long, metal box was once gray, but was now covered with rust spots and smudges of grease. It had a heavy Yale padlock looped through the front latch. "Aw, man!" Frustrated, he yanked on the lock and, surprisingly, it popped open. He slipped it from the clasp and lifted the lid.

A collection of ordinary-enough tools filled the box: a claw hammer, wire and needle-nose pliers, a staple gun, plus loose nails and bolts. The tools weren't the way he expected them to be. Dad always kept his tools clean and well-maintained. These were downright nasty. There was gummy gunk on the head and double claw of the hammer, as well as on the jaws of the pliers--brownish-red stuff, some of it running past the metal and down the rubberized handles. And the toolbox stank to the high heavens! It smelled like there was a dead mouse in there... or maybe more than one.

He lifted the handled tray and set it aside. In the lower compartment were more tools. A hacksaw, a utility knife, a Black & Decker cordless drill, and several screwdrivers. As he took the Phillips head that Mom needed, he noticed something else. Something hidden beneath a dirty, blue shop towel.

Curious, Cody lifted the cloth and held the object up to see what it was.

His heart skipped a beat—or maybe two—and he wondered if what he was looking at was actually what it seemed to be.

It was a small Gerber's baby food jar filled with a clear yellow liquid.

Floating in the middle of the fluid were two human nipples.

Startled, he quickly set the jar on the stained concrete of the garage floor. He stared at it for a few seconds, then—being the pre-adolescent boy that he was—he decided to take a second look.

It wasn't a man's nipples. They were too big. He decided they belonged to a woman instead. His best friend, Jimmy Smith, had smuggled a *Playboy* from an old Army duffle bag of his father's, so Cody knew what a naked woman looked like and how big her tits should be (they were gigantic!). The nipples in the jar were about as big as his thumb and a brownish color, not tiny and pink like his. He shook the jar a little and the plugs of flesh spun, suspended, in their liquid. The backs of them were flat and bloodless, almost blue in color. It looked as though they had been sliced off with a very sharp knife.

Cody suddenly felt a little queasy, the way he did when he ate a jumbo corndog and then rode the Scrambler at the county fair. *But... but what are they doing in here?*

They might have had some plausible reason for being in a museum or a doctor's office... but in Dad's garage?

Cody looked over at the multi-drawered tool chest on the opposite side of the room. The fact that they were all locked suddenly seemed vaguely sinister.

Frightened, he returned the jar to the bottom of the toolbox and covered it with the shop cloth. He took the screwdriver he needed, closed the metal lid, and reinserted the padlock. Then the boy quickly shoved it back beneath the work bench and left the garage.

He ran into the house, hearing Mom yelling for him down the hallway. "Cody! I really need that screwdriver!"

A moment later he reached the bathroom. Mom was in the same position, holding the shower door, looking extremely annoyed. "Where did you go? China?"

"I couldn't find one in the kitchen drawer, so I had to go looking for one." Cody held the Phillips head out to her. Like the other tools, it was covered with that yucky brown gunk. And there was something he hadn't noticed before. There was a long hair stuck to the gummy shaft of the screwdriver. A blonde hair.

Dad's hair was short and black. Mom's was red.

Mom didn't react the way he expected. Her face grew pale and her eyes widened a little. "Where did you get *that*? That's not mine."

"I had to go out to the garage to find one," he said, wondering if he'd done something wrong. "I found one of Dad's."

His mother stared at the screwdriver in his hand and swallowed dryly. "You know how your dad is. How he is when someone messes with his stuff, especially his tools."

Cody's ears reddened. "I'm sorry. I'll put it back."

"No!" Was that alarm he heard in her voice? "No. Just set it on the counter there and go find mine. It could've gotten shoved into the back of the drawer."

"Okay." Feeling kind of weird, the twelve-year-old headed back to the kitchen. He rummaged around in the junk drawer and there it was, lying in the very back, beneath a couple of old refrigerator magnets and pack of AA batteries.

When he returned to the bathroom, Mom wasn't in the same place. The shower door was leaning up against the bathroom wall and she was standing in the middle of the floor with her back turned toward the door. As though she had left the bathroom and returned only a second ago.

"Here you go, Mom," he said. "Right where you said."

She smiled and took it. "Thanks."

He looked over at the sink. The Phillips head from the garage toolbox was gone.

Cody helped his mother place the shower door back into position and she tightened the screws that held it in place. He was afraid she would fuss at him for messing around with his father's stuff, but she said nothing else about it.

"Mom?"

She turned and regarded him. "Yeah, hon?"

He almost mentioned the jar but decided not to. Not yet. "Oh... nothing."

"Cody, I got some of those popsicles you like at the grocery store," she told him. "Those big blueberry ones. We called them 'Blue-Boys' when I was growing up..."

The boy rolled his eyes. "And you waited all day for the ice cream truck, and they were only fifty cents."

Mom shook her head and laughed. "Alright, sass-pot!" Her face was pretty, for someone in her mid-thirties he supposed. But it was still paler than usual. "Why don't you get yourself one? Or get two and take one over to Jimmy's. I talked to his mother a while ago and they're back from his dentist appointment."

"Okay, Mom. Thanks."

Cody left the bathroom and his mom and dad's bedroom. He stopped by the fridge and slid two "Blue-Boys" from the box, then left the house, heralding his exit with the slapping of the screen door.

Taking Jimmy a popsicle was one reason for going next door. But there was another reason, too. One that wasn't nearly as innocent and fun.

One that almost made him feel sick to his stomach.

They were sitting in the floor of Jimmy's room, finishing up their popsicles, when Cody finally asked him.

"Uh… can I take a look at the Collection?"

Jimmy looked surprised, but pleased. "Since when are you interested in my Collection? I thought you said it was Super Sick with two capital S's."

"There's something I want to look up, that's all."

"Which one? I have five volumes, you know."

"F through I."

Jimmy nodded and went to a bookcase full of comic books, *Star Wars* figures, and some odd things, like a racoon skull and a rubber severed hand he had ordered online. He stretched while standing on his toes and took down one of the black binders that sat in a place of honor between a bloody Jason hockey mask and a Freddy clawed glove he had made out of one his dad's old Wells Lamont work gloves and set of steak knives he'd bought at Mrs. Tucker's last yard sale a few houses down.

"There you go," he said, pitching it onto his bed. "What are you interested in?"

Cody didn't answer at first. His best friend had a weird hobby. He devoured and documented anything that had to do with crime, murder, or serial killers. His infamous Collection consisted of five three-inch binders with page upon page of newspaper and magazine clippings, as well as articles and Wikipedia pages he had printed off the internet. Cody had always overlooked his pal's gruesome fascination, but most of their classmates—and even some of the teachers—regarded him as a social leper, mostly because they didn't want to hear his constant theories and forensic tidbits about Jeffery Dahmer, Richard Ramirez, or the Son of Sam.

"I'm looking for something… recent." Cody flipped through the binder. Albert Fish, Luis Garavito, Donald Henry Gaskins. He found what he was looking for between Ed Gein and H.H. Holmes.

Jimmy looked over his shoulder. "Hmmm… the Handyman Killer. Quiet an enigma. He hasn't eluded the police as long as Dennis

Rader did, but he has been active for fifteen years and, so far, no one has a clue who he is."

Cody looked at seventeen youthful faces: eight boys and nine girls. All between the ages of fourteen and twenty-one. All tortured for long periods of time and horribly mutilated by the Handyman's grisly expertise with common household tools. Most were missing for at least two or three months before their disfigured and dismembered bodies were discovered in a variety of dumping sites: country road ditches, abandoned buildings, or trash dumpsters.

Staring at the faces of the young women, Cody realized that all except one had blonde hair.

"The police think that maybe he's a construction worker," Jimmy theorized. "Or a utility worker or mechanic. Whatever he is, he sure seems to know the tools of his trade."

Tools. Cody thought about the garage a few yards from Jimmy's bedroom window. Of the gummy, brown refuse on the contents of the toolbox and that godawful stench of decay.

And the little jar containing human parts in the place of strained peas.

A couple of days passed. During that time, Cody watched his dad very closely.

His father, Harold Dawson, had always been a quiet, somber kind of guy. Cody could count on the fingers of one hand how many times his dad had laughed out loud or cracked a joke. Mostly he kept to himself, mowing and trimming the lawn, sitting in the living room watching TV—mostly the news—and puttering around the garage with one project or another. Sometimes at night he would go down to the VFW for a beer or two, or bowl with his league at Ten Pin Alleys.

Often, Cody's mom would come home from a church function or one of the crafting classes she taught at the community center and have no earthly idea where her husband was or what he was up to. He usually arrived several hours later, dark, moody and uncommunicative, giving no explanation of his whereabouts.

Out of curiosity, the boy snuck into his parents' bedroom and took down the photo albums they kept on the top shelf of the closet. He was disturbed to find that the only photographs that graced the pages were of their life beginning with Cody's birth. Before that… nothing. No childhood school pictures, no wedding photos, no vacation snapshots of Deborah and Harold Dawson before their son had come along. It was as though what had been before hadn't mattered. He looked for other things too. Report cards, high school diplomas, a marriage license, his father's military discharge papers. They were nowhere to be found… if they existed at all.

Why would his mother allow an expungement of their life before their only child's birth… unless there was control and secrecy involved?

Cody remembered how stricken his mother's face had been when she saw that screwdriver. How the blood had drained from her features and how the tool had been strangely absent when he had returned from his second visit to the junk drawer.

Maybe she knows something, he couldn't help but think. *Maybe she knows exactly who he is… and what he does when he's away from home.*

It was the Wednesday before school started when Cody Dawson discovered who the Handyman really was.

They were having a women's luncheon at the Baptist church and his mother was one of the hostesses. Cody was alone. Jimmy had gone on a summer-end daytrip to Chattanooga, so Cody hung around the house, watching TV and indulging in a lunch of Chef Boyardee spaghetti and meatballs.

He was stretched out on the living room couch when his father unexpectedly walked through the front door.

The fine hairs on the back of the twelve-year-old's neck stood up as Harold Dawson stepped inside the house and shut the door behind him. "Hi, Dad," Cody said, trying to sound like he didn't care one way or another. He laid perfectly still and didn't move a muscle.

"Is your mom still at the church?" he asked with a peculiar look on his face.

Cody nodded. "Yep. At that luncheon thing. She shouldn't be back until after two." He looked past his father at the grandfather clock in the hallway. Its ornate hands read 12:14. "You know, they have to wash dishes and clean up."

Dad said nothing, just nodded. Then he walked into the kitchen, took a frozen dinner from the freezer, and nuked it in the microwave.

Five minutes later, he left the way he came, carrying the hot dinner—Salisbury steak and mashed potatoes from the smell of it—in an oven mitt his Granny Dawson had knitted for a Christmas gift a couple of years ago. He also held can of Diet Coke in the other hand. "See you later, sport," the man called, then shut the door behind him.

Cody hopped up from the couch and went to the window. He watched as his father set the dinner and drink on the seat of his pickup truck and climbed in. The vehicle backed into the street and headed east... in the opposite direction of the gas station where Dad worked.

The boy stood in indecision for a long moment. Part of him wanted to forget his father's uncharacteristic visit and get back to his TV watching. But the other part... the part that had seemingly awakened after that gruesome discovery in the toolbox—had to know where he was going.

Cody left the house. His bike was parked against the side wall of the garage. He disengaged the kick stop and was about to follow his father's truck, when he got the urge to peek through the panes of the garage window. It was shadowy inside, but he could see the work bench on the other side. The carburetor and antifreeze jug were there, but the toolbox was gone.

The boy hit the road, pedaling as fast as he could manage. Once he reached the main road, he spotted his dad's white Chevy heading across town. Luckily, he was driving the speed limit, which was thirty-five, so Cody had a good chance of at least keeping the truck in sight.

Ten minutes later he saw his father turn off the road and into the Safe-T-Store Storage Units & U-Haul Rental. He knew the place well. His sixth-grade teacher from last year, Mrs. Baker, managed the place during the summer months.

There was no security gate like some storage facilities had, so Cody didn't have any trouble following his dad. He pedaled slowly, trying to keep out of sight, until the white pickup braked to a stop outside of a storage unit at the very back of the lot. Cody parked his bike and peered around the far corner. His father took a keyring from his pants pocket and unlocked the built-in lock on one of the unit doors. Then he rolled the door upward, stepped inside with the dinner and drink, and rolled it back down again.

Quickly, Cody ran along the long building of units, hoping... praying... that the man didn't leave before he got there. He finally stood at the unit door. The number painted on the segmented steel read 208.

Cody heard noises on the other side, but couldn't quite make them out. Despite the chance of discovery, he knew he had to know what was taking place inside. Quietly, he pressed one ear firmly against the door.

He heard his father talking low and calmly. He also heard another sound, a voice muffled by some obstruction. It didn't belong to a man, but a woman. Harold Dawson continued, soothingly. Then there was a harsh sound... like someone pulling away a strip of tape. A sharp gasp of pain followed. The woman's voice suddenly grew clearer. She didn't speak. It was worse than that. Although he couldn't quite make it out, he believed that she was crying and pleading for mercy.

Cody heard a vehicle and pulled his ear away for a moment. An SUV with a mattress and box springs bungeed to the roof passed the gap between two rows of units and disappeared. He listened again. Things had quieted down. The girl still cried but it was more subdued. Cody heard a fizzy pop... the can of soda being opened.

The boy knew it was time to go when he heard the girl whimper, followed by the sound of tape being pulled from the roll. Cody ran down the long row of units and reached the end just as he heard the door roll up with a clatter. He ducked around the cinderblock wall and peered back around the corner. His father stepped out, lowered the door, and locked it. He walked to a trash can nearby, intending to dump the soda can and plastic dinner plate. Deciding differently, he tossed the trash onto the seat of the pickup, then climbed in himself. The girl's DNA was probably on the mouth of the Coke can and the frozen dinner tray.... saliva or snot... or maybe even her blood.

He watched as the truck left. It circled around several rows of units and exited the way it had entered. Cody watched until his dad was out of sight, heading in the direction of the Exxon station. He waited five minutes, but it seemed like forever. Then he rode his bike to the front office, took a deep breath to calm himself, and walked inside.

Mrs. Baker seemed pleased to see him. "Well, hi there, Cody. Have you enjoyed your summer vacation?"

Cody smiled. "Yes, ma'am."

"Are you ready for school to start?"

Cody frowned. "No, ma'am!"

The teacher laughed. "To tell the truth, me neither." She set down the Amish romance paperback she had been reading. "What are doing out here, halfway across town?"

"My Dad sent me to fetch something in his unit, but I forgot the key," he told her, as straight-faced as he could manage. "You don't have a spare one I could borrow for a minute, do you?"

Mrs. Baker turned toward a peg board with several dozen keys hanging there. "Sure. What number was it again?"

Cody's heart pounded so hard that he was afraid the woman might hear it. "It's 208."

She found the key and handed it to him. "There you go. Just bring it back when you're finished."

"Yes, ma'am." Cody left the office and ducked out of sight. He stood behind the office, doubled over, with his hands on his knees, breathing deeply. Then he straightened up and looked toward the end unit on Row 2.

Oh Lord… please… I don't want to go down there.

But he knew that he had to.

He jumped on his ten-speed and pedaled past the long line of doors. It was the longest bicycle ride he had ever taken in his life. When he got there, he stood in front of the door of 208 for what seemed an eternity. Then he inserted the key into the lock and heaved the door upward on its tracks.

The brilliant summer sun flooded into the eight-by-twelve chamber, revealing all that was there.

Chamber was the correct word. If you put the word "torture" in front of it.

A number of pullies had been anchored into the ceiling of the storage unit and, from them, dangled heavy chains. Some sported shackles, while others were tipped with grappling or meat hooks. A heavy wooden work bench, completely stained in congealed blood, held a heavy-duty vice on one corner. A number of tools were scattered across the countertop, including the old toolbox Cody had discovered several days ago. Along the opposite wall were larger tools: a sledgehammer, a rotary saw, and a chainsaw. All were stained with blood and bits of flesh and hair.

A single bank of fluorescent lights—identical to the ones in Dad's garage—was connected to a small generator. It was apparent that the noisy work was done in the dead of night, hours after the Safe-T-Store had closed and there was no one around to hear what was taking place in Unit 208.

A whimper drew his attention to the back wall. What he saw there scared the living shit out of him.

It was a teenage girl, maybe sixteen years old. She was blonde and had probably been pretty at one time... maybe even beautiful. But that was all gone now. The Handyman had done his work well and it showed.

With the sun glaring through the open doorway, Cody expected the girl's eyes to be tightly clenched. But that was impossible. Someone had cut away her eyelids. Her baby blue eyes were horribly wide and bloodshot. She was covered in blood. Her McDonald's uniform was tattered and her exposed breasts and slender arms were covered with patterns cut into her flesh: a pentagram, random numbers and letters, a crude drawing of a skull with a wreath of daisies around its crown, several crisscross games of tic-tac-toe here and there. There were other scars, too. Cigarette burns and puncture wounds from something long and blunt. Maybe a Phillips head screwdriver.

She couldn't talk because her lower face was sealed shut by a broad strip of silver duct tape. The naked bones of her cheeks and lower jaw told him that—if he'd had the nerve to remove the gag—there wouldn't have been any lips, either bottom or top.

The girl wasn't tied up with ropes or anything, which puzzled the boy at first. Then he saw what confined her. Half-shackles of heavy iron secured her narrow wrists to the concrete floor, fastened there with long masonry bolts. Only three of her ten fingers remained intact.

Abruptly, Cody Dawson turned and puked up his Chef Boyardee onto the warm pavement that stretched between the storage units. He gagged and heaved until nothing more remained in his stomach, then he thought of the girl—no, the *thing*—imprisoned inside and he retched again until his throat was raw and his nose began to bleed.

He jumped on his bike and made it back to the office in a matter of seconds. He burst through the door and stood there for a long moment, unable to speak. Mrs. Baker stared at him like he was a stranger... stared at his pale and terrified face... at the fresh puke that wreathed his mouth and speckled the front of his t-shirt.

"Cody... what... what's wrong?"

"Call... call the police," he stammered, trying hard not to cry. "Call 9-1-1. Something... *terrible...* has happened at Unit 208."

Alarm crossed Mrs. Baker's face and she took a step toward the end of the counter. Cody jumped in front of her, blocking her way. "Don't go down there, Mrs. Baker," he begged. "Please! If you do, you'll have nightmares for the rest of your life. Believe me... I'm not kidding."

The woman could tell that the boy was telling the truth. "What's happened?"

"The Handyman," was all that he could manage to say.

"Oh, dear Lord," she breathed.

As Mrs. Baker began to dial, Cody turned and ran out the door. He heard her call out to him, urging him to stay put, but he ignored her. He jumped on his bike and pedaled into the street, heading back across town.

"Mom!" Cody yelled as he burst through the utility room door. "Mom... where are you?"

He knew she was home. Her car was parked in the driveway. As he ran through the kitchen and started down the hallway, he heard the shower in the bathroom that adjoined his parents' bedroom. The sound of running water didn't surprise him. His mother usually took a shower after a particularly active day.

He stepped into the bedroom and stood there, trembling. "Mom?"

"Cody?" she called. "What is it, hon?"

"Mom... I..." The boy's heart pounded harder than he could ever remember. *How am I going to tell her?* He took a deep breath, held it, let it out. "Something... something *horrible* has happened!"

The water suddenly stopped. "What, Cody? What happened?"

He felt dizzy, as though he was about to faint. "It's... it's Dad."

Cody heard the shower door open. A moment later, his mother stepped into the bedroom. She was dripping wet, holding a thick terrycloth towel in front of her body. It barely covered her, from collarbone to the tops of her thighs.

She stared at him, alarmed. "What... what about your dad?"

He didn't want to tell her... more than *anything*, he didn't want to tell her. But he did.

"Dad..." Cody gasped, "He's done something awful! There's a storage unit across town and... and..."

The twelve-year-old stopped talking. His mother's face had turned as white as flour. Her arms slowly dropped to her sides and the towel fell away, pooling around her feet. She stood there completely naked in front of him.

Her plump breasts stared blindly at him.

For they had no nipples.

Suddenly, he knew. He began to cry. "Oh, Mom... why did he... why did he do that to you?"

A smile crossed Debbie Dawson's pretty face. It was the smile he had known all his life. It was Mom's smile. But her eyes... her eyes were dead. They stared at him like two smooth, black stones. No love... no affection... no concern. No feeling at all.

"I wish you hadn't found out until you were older," she said. Then she turned and walked to her cherrywood dresser. Opened a side drawer. Took out a long wood-handled file... one that had been meticulously ground down to a wickedly sharp point. The diagonal lines of the flat blade were tacky with dried blood and tiny slivers of splintered bone.

Then she started walking toward him.

Cody stumbled backward, more confused than he had ever been in his young life. Before he reached the bedroom door, he bumped into something. Or someone.

He looked up and saw his dad standing over him... holding a 9mm pistol at arm's length.

The muzzle of the gun wasn't directed at him, however.

"Stop, Debbie," said Harold Dawson in a flat, emotionless voice. "Please... sweetheart... just stop."

Mom... Debbie... wouldn't listen. Her smile broadened, while her eyes grew darker and deader. She raised the file and kept coming.

"We agreed," he said. "A long time ago. Not the boy. Anyone but the boy."

Debbie Dawson made a sound, down deep in her throat. A giggle... a sob... Cody couldn't tell for sure. Her pace quickened.

There was eight feet of space between them now. Seven… six…

An explosion like cannon fire went off in Cody's ears. An ugly red hole appeared between his mother's breasts. She staggered back a few steps and looked down at the bullet wound. She raised her free hand and probed the hole in her flesh… stuck her finger inside. Withdrew it and stared at the blood on her fingertip, then raised it to her lips.

Dad fired again. The second round struck her squarely in the forehead. The family photos on the wall behind her—tastefully framed and proudly displayed—were suddenly speckled with blood and pulpy bits of brain.

Cody watched as mother fell backward and landed heavily upon the carpet. She twitched once… twice… then grew motionless. That silly smile was still—and forever—on her face.

Frightened, Cody fled from his father. He crouched at the base of the chest of drawers a few feet away and cowered. "Please… please, Dad. Don't."

His father stared at him for a long moment. He lowered his gun and tossed it across the room. It bounced once and landed in the threshold of the bathroom doorway.

"I'm not going to shoot you, son," he said. He stepped over his wife's dead body and sat down heavily on the end of the big king-size bed he had shared with her for fourteen years.

Cody stared at him. He wanted to cut and run… downstairs, out of the house, into the street. But he remained where he was. "Why… why did you do that to her? To Mom? Why did you cut off her… her…?"

Harold Dawson raised his head and regarded his son. His eyes were full of pain. "Cody… I didn't do that." He stared at his wife. "She did… before we were married."

"But… but I found them… in your toolbox."

"Son, that toolbox wasn't mine. It was *hers*."

The boy didn't think he could feel any sicker than he had at the storage unit across town, but he did now. "So, you're not the…" He faltered to digest what he now knew. "That girl… clamped to the floor…"

Dad nodded. "It was her. Her all along."

"All of them?"

"All of them… and then some."

Cody straightened up but didn't move toward his father. He simply stood where he was. "But you knew. Knew that she was…"

"The Handyman?" His father's voice was flat, toneless. "From the very beginning."

"But... *why?*"

"You're too young to understand, Cody," he told him. "How a man can love a woman so much that he'd put up with and allow anything. Even embrace a very real and damning piece of Hell on Earth... just to be close to her."

They could hear sirens in the distance.

"They'll be here soon and you won't see me again for a while. Could be for the last time. Your aunt and uncle in Virginia will take good care of you."

Debbie jerked and sighed deeply.

"She's alive!" Cody moaned.

"No," his father assured. "It's just her body getting comfortable with death, her systems shutting down for good. I've seen it happen before."

Cody knew that he had. Probably more times than he wanted to admit.

"They'll put me away for being an accessory. Not for participating... I was never there when she did it. Just showed up to show a little kindness before and to clean up afterward. They'll probably want to pen it on me at first, but your mom's diaries will set things straight. She had a lot of them. From the early days... when she was in high school... until now. I never read them. She encouraged it... but I never could bring myself to."

Outside, the sirens grew shrill and loud. Soon the flashing of blue lights reflected through the bedroom windows and colored the walls.

"I'm sorry, son. Sorry for this whole ugly mess. Always remember... I love you." He stretched out his arms, but they remained empty.

Cody wanted to return the sentiment, but it simply wasn't in him.

"Get in that closet there and stay put," his father instructed. "I don't want you out here... in case somebody comes looking for the Handyman and loses it."

The boy nodded and stepped into the closet. Tears blurred his last glimpse of Harold Dawson before the door closed. Through the distortion he thought he saw his dad smile for the first time in a very long time.

Standing in the darkness, hearing the drumming of feet in the hallway and excited voices, Cody wondered how a boy's carefree life could be flipped upside down and turned inside out in a matter of days.

All because of a baby food jar in an old, worn-out toolbox.

A week following his twenty-second birthday, Cody Dawson accompanied his new bride, Cindy, to Washington D.C.

It was their honeymoon and neither one had ever been to the nation's capital before. Cody had just graduated from college and was starting a new sales position with a pharmaceutical company in Richmond. Cindy was starting a nurse internship at a hospital, while still going to school part-time. She had hopes of becoming a nurse practitioner in a year or two.

They saw all the sights. The Capitol Building, the monuments, the memorials. They even took a tour of the White House. Then, while making the rounds at the Smithsonian museums, Cody saw the sign and froze in his tracks.

"Come on," urged Cindy. "Let's grab a bite to eat and then head over to the National Gallery. There's some paintings I've always wanted to see."

But Cody didn't move. He just looked at the banner that hung in front of the Museum of American History. The banner that boasted several infamous faces... and one familiar one.

"You're going in, aren't you?"

"Yes."

She gripped his hand firmly, lovingly. "Do you want me to come?"

Her husband smiled and kissed her on the forehead. "I need to do this alone."

Cindy nodded. "I understand."

After a moment's hesitation, he climbed the steps and went inside. Ten years had placed a comfortable distance between this afternoon and that awful life-altering one, but stepping into the museum's American Crime and Punishment exhibit closed that gap very quickly, almost jarringly so.

He passed the first few exhibits by without interest. The Old West... Billy the Kid, Jesse James, John Wesley Hardin. The Gangster and Bank Robbery Era... Al Capone, Dillinger, Bonnie and Clyde.

It was when he got to Mass Murderers and Serial Killers that he walked slowly and took his time.

The really infamous ones were first. Charles Whitman's Texas Tower rifle. John Wayne Gacy's clown costumes and prison paintings. Ted Bundy's little tan Volkswagen Beetle.

Then he turned a corner in the maze of partitions, and he was there.

Several people were standing around a glass display case. Cody stepped up as a couple of them moved on. He stared at the rusty, beaten and battered toolbox that sat on display. Its lid was folded back and its contents were visible, for all to see. The hammer, the hacksaw, the pliers, both screwdrivers... Phillips head and flat head. The tools looked too clean. They had obviously been cleaned of their grisly reddish-brown patina. But you could still see traces of what had been there... if you knew where to look.

He stared at the toolbox for a while, then lifted his gaze to a small shelf mounted on the wall above the case. It held a glass box with a single object inside.

Cody stared at the baby food jar with the two plugs of flesh floating inside, obscenely fascinating and perfectly preserved.

A small placard above the case gave insight to one of the most disturbing items in the history of American crime.

The Nipples of Deborah Ann Dawson

After years of torture and sexual abuse by male family members, Deborah Dawson severed her nipples in an act of self-mutilation on the night of her sixteenth birthday.

It was the beginning of a disturbing double-life that spanned nearly twenty years. Housewife and mother by day, cold-blooded serial killer by night. Known as the Handyman Killer for her proficiency with common tools, Dawson was responsible for the torture and murders of 26 known victims... 15 women and 11 men, all between the ages of 14 and 21. Her crimes were aided and concealed by her husband, Harold.

"She sure was a sick bitch, wasn't she?" said a young man standing beside him, shaking his head with disgust.

Cody studied the large poster of the Handyman posted next to the exhibit. A fresh-faced, red-haired woman in her early thirties, wearing a yellow dress and matching heels, posing for a quick photo in front of the church she had attended most of her life. Cody stared into that face and remembered. The trips to Florida and building sandcastles together on the beach. The scent of chocolate chip cookies fresh from the oven and biscuits and bacon for breakfast. A cold compress and her motherly concern during nights of fever and sickness. A gentle kiss goodnight on Christmas Eve before Santa put the presents under the tree.

Cody turned to the boy and nodded. "Yes," he said softly, "she sure was."

But she was Mom.

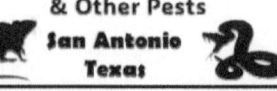

ABOUT THE AUTHOR

Ronald Kelly was born November 20, 1959, in Nashville, Tennessee, where he was raised a Southern Baptist. He attended Pegram Elementary School and Cheatham County Central High School (both in Ashland City, Tennessee) before starting his writing career.

Ronald Kelly began his writing career in 1986 and quickly sold his first short story, "Breakfast Serial," to Terror Time Again magazine. His first novel, Hindsight was released by Zebra Books in 1990. His audiobook collection, Dark Dixie: Tales of Southern Horror, was on the nominating ballot of the 1992 Grammy Awards for Best Spoken Word or Non-Musical Album. Zebra published seven of Ronald Kelly's novels from 1990 to 1996. Ronald's short fiction work has been published by Cemetery Dance, Borderlands 3, Deathrealm, Dark at Heart, Hot Blood: Seeds of Fear, and many more. After selling hundreds of thousands of books, the bottom dropped out of the horror market in 1996. So, when Zebra dropped their horror line in October 1996, Ronald Kelly stopped writing for almost ten years and worked various jobs including welder, factory worker, production manager, drugstore manager, and custodian.

In 2006, Ronald Kelly started writing again. Since then, he has written and published several new novels (Hell Hollow, Restless Shadows, and The Buzzard Zone), numerous short story collections, and has become an elder statesman of Southern-Fried Horror in his chosen genre. In 2021, his collection of extreme horror tales, The Essential Sick Stuff, won the Splatterpunk Award for Best Collection. He is currently working on The Saga of Dead-Eye, a five-volume horror western series.

Ronald Kelly currently lives in a backwoods hollow in Brush Creek, Tennessee, with his wife and young'uns.

BOOK LIST

Novels

Blood Kin
Father's Little Helper (re-released as *Twelve Gauge*)
Fear (Author's Preferred Edition)
Hell Hollow
Hindsight
Moon of the Werewolf (re-released as Undertaker's Moon)
Pitfall
Restless Shadows
Something Out There (re-released as *The Dark'Un*)
The Buzzard Zone
The China Doll
The Possession (re-released as Burnt Magnolia)
The Saga of Dead-Eye, Book One: Vampires, Zombies, & Mojo Men
*The Saga of Dead-Eye, Book Two: Werewolves, Swamp Critters, &
Hellacious Haints*
Timber Gray

Novellas

Flesh Welder

Collections

Curious about other Crossroad Press books?
Stop by our site:
www.crossroadpress.com
We offer quality writing
in digital, audio, and print formats.

www.ingramcontent.com/pod-product-compliance
Lightning Source LLC
Chambersburg PA
CBHW022025170626
46808CB00003B/1059